My Wicked Step The Diary

First published 2
Go∕

GoApe Books is the junior fiction imprint of

Monkey Island Publishing
Dairy Cottage
Hurgill Road
Richmond
North Yorkshire
DL10 4SZ

Text copyright © 2017 Karen Langtree
Illustrations copyright © 2017 Gill McLean
The moral rights of Karen Langtree and Gill McLean have been asserted

ISBN 978-0-9930636-4-0

To
Martha.

Wicked Wishes !

Karen

A Letter from Lou...

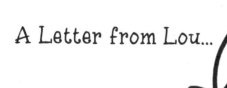

Hi,

I hope you enjoy a sneaky peek into my very personal diary, from the year I met my wicked stepmother. If you have read the previous book about me, you'll love the fact that you can read so much more detail about other things that happened, and get right inside my mind.

Oooooh!

If you didn't read the previous book about me, don't worry, all the juicy gossip is here in my diary.

Just in case you're new to text-speak, here's a list of what it all means, when you come across it in Zoe's and my messages.

Enjoy my diary!

Lou

IKR	= I know, right?	PCM	= please call me
SMH	= shaking my head	NMH	= nodding my head
BFF	= Best Friend Forever	TTYL	= talk to you later
K	= okay	sKK	= it's okay
LMK	= let me know	PAP	= post a picture
BTW	= by the way	ROFL	= roll on the floor laughing

Saturday 13th January

Dear Diary,

You think my life is just a silly fairy-tale, don't you? After all, wicked stepmothers are one of the main ingredients. But this is no fairytale; this is my life! My REAL life! And wicked stepmothers do exist. I've just got one. Her name is Eve.

How can I describe today? I mean, if I had to sum it up in one word.

None of these comes close. There we were, thinking we were just ordinary kids, me twelve, Nat eight, getting on with normal, boring life. You know, school, homework, friend hassles, avoiding bedroom tidying, that sort of stuff...

Then,

It all kicks off. It's like someone sumo-wrestled me to the ground, without even asking me for a fight! I don't know why sumo-wrestlers popped into my mind there... Anyway, here are the details...

Nat and I are early risers, so we slipped downstairs, quietly, as usual, so as not to disturb Mum and Dad. (Considerate.) We like watching TV together when no one's about. (Sisterly love.) Okay, I admit it, I still like watching some of her programmes, even though technically I've grown out of them. I will only admit that to you, Dear Diary, so keep it to yourself

Nat was snuggled up with Poops (yes, that's what she called her toy dog when she was two) and I was messaging my friends to see if anyone was up yet. No replies. No surprise there! So, I went into the kitchen to get some cereal. Dad was sitting there, drinking coffee. That was the first weird thing. Mum and Dad rarely get up before ten on Saturdays. He was wearing an old T-shirt and jeans. His mousy hair was sticking out, like a loo brush that's had a nasty collision with an electric socket. He had big black bags under his eyes.

'Having a bad-hair day, Dad?' said witty old me. 'What are you doing up so early, anyway?'

He gave me this kind of watery

smile and tried to laugh, except it came out like he'd gulped his coffee down the wrong way. 'Alright, Lou?'

Am I alright? 'Yeah Dad,' I said, 'but what about you?'

He suddenly realised how odd it was, him sitting there, at seven thirty on a Saturday, looking like a scarecrow and drinking coffee. He gulped another mouthful. 'Oh, I guess this seems a bit... hmmm,' he said vaguely, glancing down at his clothes. 'I'm just waiting for your Mum, and then we've... I've got something to tell you.'

'What?'

'Erm... best wait 'til Mum comes down.'

'Why?'

He did this strange thing with his mouth and eyebrows, didn't say anything and for a second he looked like he might cry.

I shrugged my shoulders and turned back to my phone. I messaged Zoe:

> My Dad is weird! 😞

She didn't reply, of course, because she would still be asleep for another four hours yet!

I took Nat some breakfast (note: kind sister) and we watched TV. I was laughing at this cartoon thingy I used to watch when I was her age. It was still funny (but no telling anyone, Diary). I forgot about Dad, until Mum appeared at the living room door. She wasn't in her dressing gown. She had jeans and a big cardi on. I wondered if they were going out somewhere, and we were going to have to go with them. She looked tired.

'Okay girls?' she said.

'Yeah,' I said, and smiled at her. She fake-smiled back, then went to the kitchen. Nat never took her eyes off the screen, but I was wondering what was going on. Both parents out of bed. It was only seven thirty something. That's not natural.

'Don't you think that's weird, Nat?' I said. She didn't reply. 'Nat!' I kicked her feet from the other end of the sofa.

'Hey! Get off.' She kicked me back. (Sisterly love)

'Nat, Mum and Dad are up. Something's going on.'

'What? I'm trying to watch this,' she scowled, turning the TV up.

I messaged Zoe again:

Get up y lazy blob! Need to talk

Mum came back. 'Girls, turn the TV off, your Dad and I need to tell you something.' She headed back to the kitchen.

'Come on,' I said, swiping the remote from Nat and switching the TV off. She protested, but I dragged her off the sofa. 'Come on. Mum and Dad are being weird. Something's up.'

I must admit, I already had a bad feeling. You know when you feel like there's a gremlin in your stomach, pinching your insides, then laughing

8

about it? I thought perhaps they were going to tell us that Dad had lost his job, or we weren't going on holiday this year, or even that someone was seriously ill. I really, really never dreamt what it was they were actually going to say.

Nat and I stood in the kitchen doorway, leaning on the doorposts. Mum stood propped against the work surface, and Dad was still sitting where I'd found him when I first came into the kitchen. There was this awkward silence, as we looked at each other warily. Mum glared at Dad, and I suddenly realised he was in big trouble. But what did that have to do with us? They argue a bit, but normally upstairs, or with the door shut. She never usually drags us into it. I hoped she wasn't going to make us take sides because I was NOT doing it. He never looked at her, so he hadn't got a clue about the 'glare vibes' she was sending him.

'Well, Mike,' she snapped, 'Are you going to speak?' Dad rubbed his hand across his face. He looked at Nat and I, like we were foxes and he was a rabbit, about to be devoured.

I was thinking there must be something up with Dad. He was sick. Cancer. Only weeks to live!

'Dad!' I said, thinking, 'Come on! Just tell us!' So, he did. He simply blurted it out.

'I'm leaving.'

Two words. That's all it took, and my whole world collapsed, as if someone just blew me up like a derelict building. I started to hyper-thingy-whatsit. I couldn't speak, because I didn't even see it coming, but now it

9

was so obvious. Everyone has this thing about your life flashing before you when you're about to die. But mine started to replay right there. Scenes that hadn't meant anything to me before... Mum and Dad getting at each other, never sitting together on the sofa, Mum bashing his plate down on the tea table, Dad coming in late most nights and watching TV, Mum stomping upstairs, slamming doors.

I was drawn back from the nightmare when Nat said, innocently, 'Leaving where Dad? Are you getting a new job or something?'

The gremlins suddenly started jumping up and down, cackling hysterically, and I thought, 'I'm going to be sick.' I wanted to shake Nat, and tell her not to be so stupid. Then I wanted to hug her, and tell her that he was leaving us; he was splitting up with Mum. But I still couldn't speak. Dad also seemed paralysed. Suddenly, he began to sob and buried his face in his hands. We'd never seen Dad cry before. Nat ran over to him and put her arms round his shoulders.

'Daddy, what's wrong? ...Why are you crying?'

Then Mum started this slow clapping. Eh? What was she doing? 'Oh, sensitively handled, Mike! Well done!' She prised Nat from Dad's shoulders and sat down opposite him, with Nat on her knee. I pulled off some sheets of kitchen roll and gave them to Dad, who was now wiping his nose with the back of his hand.

He began to try and explain. 'I'm so sorry, girls. I'm not doing this very well.' He blew his nose and I don't know why, but I suddenly felt like I was in an American sitcom, with canned audience laughter in the background. (Why would I think that? It wasn't in the least bit funny!) 'I'm not going to be living with you and Mum anymore.

I'm moving out this morning. Your mum and I have had a long talk about this and it's for the best. You see, your mum and I haven't been getting on very well for a long time...'

Yes, I get that!

'We've tried to work things out. We really have.'

Mum made a noise like a constipated camel at this point.

Then, the even bigger bombshell, if there could be one. Dad carried on. 'And... I've met someone else...' (he stuttered a lot here.) 'Someone... who I... I want to live with now and your Mum and I... well we... we love you both as much as ever; I want you to know that, more than anything else. That will never change. Never! But ... now, I can't stay here any more. I'll still be able to see you lots, I just won't live here anymore. I'll still be your Dad. And I'll love you just as much as ever.'

Finally, he finished rambling. Mum scowled at him. I stared at him, but tears silently slid down my face. I could taste them.

Nat was crying too. Then the questions started. 'Why don't you want to live with us anymore, Dad? And what's wrong with Mum? She's nice. You do love her. You married her so you must love her...'

He said he was sorry, again, and that he loved us, blah,blah, blah. But he was still going to leave us.

'Are you going to get a divorce?' I asked, sniffing back the snot.

He said yes, squeezing my hand and looking like a pathetic puppy who's just wee'd all over your shoe.

Mum came over all matter-of-fact at this point. (She was the only one not crying, which I didn't get). She decided it was time to explain some practical things to us. 'Your Dad is going to live across the other side of town, in Queen Elizabeth Road, near Jubilee Park. We've agreed for now that you will go and stay with him for one day and night at the weekends. We've got his phone number, so you can ring him if you want to talk to him anytime. Now I think you should go Mike, so the girls and I can get our heads sorted out.' She didn't even look at him; she just waved her hand in the direction of the door.

He stood up and kissed Nat. He tried to do the same to me, but I shrugged him off even though I just wanted to cling to him forever, and scream,

'DON'T GO!'

Nat clung to him, burying her face in his T-shirt, sobbing. Dad was sniffing and wiping his face with his hand. Mum pulled Nat away from him.

'Just go!' she snapped.

'Daddy!' Natalie wailed, reaching for him.

He left the kitchen, and I felt so sick. I wanted to

speak, but I couldn't. I put my hand to my throat, as if trying to release the words. He hurried up the stairs to get his things. I looked at Mum, who had gathered Nat on to her knee. Nat was just wailing, 'Daddy, Daddy,' over and over again. Mum stroked her hair, and rocked her, staring at nothing. Still no tears. Her face was like stone. I flung my arms around them both. Nat kept catching her breath as her sobs gradually got further and further apart, until eventually they stopped. No one spoke for what seemed like forever.

Suddenly Mum shook her head, as if she had just realised how to chase the whole mess away.

'Okay,' she said, 'I know we're all feeling really awful right now, and the situation is rubbish, but we can't sit here crying all day. So, there's only one thing to cheer us up: McDonald's breakfast! Come on, let's get dressed and go.'

'But what about Dad?' I asked. 'He's still here.'

'We'll say goodbye, then we'll go.'

I wandered off in a daze, to get dressed. Another weird thing. McDonald's, right now? What was Mum thinking of?

Dad stood at the door, fifteen minutes later.

'Bye.' He tried to smile. He was about to hug us, but Mum shook her head at him. 'I'll call you. See you soon. It won't seem long; promise.'

Nat flung her arms round him, crying for him to stay, begging Mum to make him stay. Mum's face was grim. She just sat on the stairs, watching, pressing her lips into a tight white line. Dad prised Nat from his body with my help. I didn't know what to say. Everything I could think of seemed useless. I'm not one for outbursts in public. I save those for private. Like here, in this diary.

Insensitive
Stupid Selfish!

We watched him drive off, then I closed the door. My face was a sticky mass of snot and tears. Nat was sobbing again and banging on the door. And now, finally, Mum began to cry. We're not used to seeing her cry. She always hides her emotions from us (which I think is also stupid). I felt angry with her, I don't know why. It was Dad who'd left. Then she whispered, 'Sorry, sorry,' over and over again, and started rocking on the bottom step. We just hugged her. Even Nat stopped crying to be strong for Mum right then.

*

At nine thirty I messaged Zoe:

> **In Maccy D's and my Dad's just left us!!!!**

Still no reply. Arggghhhh!

Nat had a Happy Meal, I had cheeseburger and fries and Mum just had fries. So much for a big breakfast. Nobody wanted one. Actually, did anybody really want to be here right now? Mum sucked each fry for ages before she swallowed it. If we did that she'd say, 'That's horrible. Eat properly.' But she was in another zone. The toys in the Happy Meal were from the latest Disney film, and normally Nat would be excited to see what she'd got. But today she wasn't bothered about it. There were lots of families around us having a good time. I noticed a few kids with just their dads, and wondered if they were visiting for the weekend. They didn't look as happy, to me, as the kids with both parents.

'Mum, will we have to move house?' Nat asked.

'No, love.'

'Will I still be able to go to Brownies on Fridays? Dad usually takes me.' Nat said.

'Yes, love. We'll work something out, don't worry.'

There was a pause. 'Will we still have th' same last name as Dad?'

Mum bristled. 'Yes, Natalie, of course you will.'

Another pause. Then I said, 'Who's this woman, Dad's met? When will we have to meet her?'

Mum got really shirty at that point. 'Oh, I don't know. Some floozy. She's called Eve or Evie or something like that. Can we drop it now?'

We didn't say much after that, for a long time.

'So, how are you getting on with that Science project, Lou?' Mum said, suddenly.

'Okay,' I replied. Pause. We slurped our drinks.

'Nat, do you want to have Katie round for tea this week?' Mum asked.

'No thanks.' Another pause and more slurping.

'Well, what shall we do tomorrow?' Mum said. 'How about the cinema?'

Nat and I looked at each other, as if Mum was a bit crazy, then shook our heads. Mum reverted to silent staring.

After McDonald's, Mum said, 'Let's go shopping.' So, we trailed round lots of clothes shops. We got some very nice tops and Nat got some expensive trainers. Mum said I could have some too, but I didn't really want any. Mum bought herself a new bag. It was dinky and sparkly. But none of us were particularly enjoying ourselves.

Finally, my phone pinged.

Zoe: Zowzers! 😵

(Zoe likes making up weird words she beginning with Z. She refuses to use OMG. Everyone does it!)

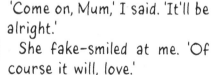

Zoe again: Your Dad left??? WHY? What's your Mum say?
Me: Got another woman. Not much
Zoe: Zeepers! Bad news
Me: Could say that. Mum's got us out shopping
Zoe: Getting loads of stuff? PAP
Me: No. Just want to go home
Zoe: Yeah 🙁

But Mum wanted to go to Pizza Hut for tea, even though it was only four o'clock. We sat in there for ages, getting refills of coke and lemonade.

'Can we go now, Mum?' asked Nat.

'Yes love, where shall we go?' she said, trying to muster some enthusiasm.

'Home,' we said together.

'Oh,' sighed Mum. 'Yes, of course. Is that the time, we've been out for ages, haven't we?'

'Come on, Mum,' I said. 'It'll be alright.'

She fake-smiled at me. 'Of course it will, love.'

Not sure I even believe that myself!

Monday 15th January:

Dear Diary,

All day yesterday Mum was on another planet. She cooked, ironed and talked like a zombie. Nat spent the day watching DVDs and asking if she could ring Dad. He had rung on Saturday night but Mum wouldn't let her ring him now. Nat got cross with Mum and refused to speak to her. I had to relay messages between them. I got annoyed with the two of them, so in the afternoon I retreated to my room to message Zoe and read what I had written to you, on Saturday, my beloved Diary. I'm still in shock, even though I know this happens all the time to people. Why do I feel so bad? How could Dad be so selfish? He's putting some woman before us. He can't really love us if he can put his love-life first. I hate him. I don't ever want to see him again!!!!!

Sorry Diary. I didn't mean to treat you harshly and slam you shut like that. You are my trusted companion who never tells my secrets to anyone. I just had to have a little cry into my pillow so no one could hear me. But that's made me feel a bit better. So here are my rational thoughts.

I don't hate him, if I'm honest (and I'm always honest with you). I just can't get my head round what he's done. I still love him. He's my Dad. But the whole thing stinks. Nat is upset. Mum is behaving weirdly. It's all gone wrong. I hate it!

Today we went to school as normal, except of course it wasn't 'normal.' Mum came with us to speak to Nat's head teacher and my head of house about our 'situation,' as she called it. First, we called at Greenfield Primary. I stayed in the car while Mum went in with Nat. It seemed to take ages. I was getting fidgety. I hate being late for form. Everyone stares at you like you're an alien, when you walk in. Then they whisper about you.

Eventually she took me on to St. Aidan's. I wished the ground would swallow me, going in with Mum. Honestly, she has no idea how embarrassing that is. She took no notice of my hints about how it might be better if she just phoned, and Mr. Dyer would be REALLY BUSY first thing. But, no, she had to do it her way.

I was late for form. And guess what? Yep, everyone stared and whispered. I tried to ignore them and homed in on Zoe, Meg and Alice. Zoe is not like you, Dear Diary. She had already blabbed everything to them. Not that I really minded because they were nice to me all day. Alice bought me a donut at lunchtime and Meg kept asking if I needed a hug. They asked loads of questions though and I got a bit fed up of that. Especially Alice; she goes on and on and on and on. (Thanks for the donut though.)

My form teacher, Miss Lowe, had obviously been told why I was late because she asked me to stay back after registration for a chat. More dirty looks from the whisperers! She was lovely though and told me I could talk to her any time. And she said if I found it difficult to concentrate on homework, not to worry about it this week. (Tempting!)

At break, Zoe and I managed to get rid of Alice and Meg, and found a corner in the courtyard by ourselves. She wasn't shocked or anything because she's lived with her Mum and her Mum's boyfriend, Rick, since she was five. Her Dad left them for someone else and she doesn't see much of him now. I had loads of questions for her.

'Did you see your Dad much at the start?'

'Yeah! I think so. It seems ages ago now.'

'Don't you miss him?'

'Nah, not really. He just messes things up when he turns up, once in a blue moon. He never lets Mum know, he just comes round and demands that I drop everything and go to his house. Well I don't need that kind of hassle in my life!'

I had this picture of Zoe's mum standing there with her hands on her hips, shouting, 'I don't need that kind of hassle in my life!' at Zoe's dad.

'Anyway, I get on much better with Rick, he's a real laugh.'

'Isn't your dad living with someone different now?'

'Yeah! That woman! She is the pits!' (Sounded like Zoe's mum again!) 'She once came round our house with my dad and shouted some really bad stuff at Mum. She was calling her 'effing' this and 'effing' that. Mum was in tears. Rick came in and chucked them out. He nearly punched my dad but Mum grabbed his arm. She was going 'he's not worth it Rick, don't hit him. He'll get you locked up.' When they'd gone, she said I was never going to Dad's again while that tart was around.'

'And have you never been since?'

'Yeah! After a few months, Mum forgot and let me go next time Dad came barging in. He said if she didn't, he'd get the law on her and that fathers have rights too. Blah, blah, blah!'

I could have talked for ages, but the bell went and we had to go. It was good talking to Zoe because she understands what I am going through. I know that you do too, Diary, but I needed someone to talk back to me as well. Hope you don't mind.

Tart

Toad's Eyeballs!

Dear Diary,

Ha ha ha! Like the title? Got you wondering what I'm going to tell you, hasn't it?

I've done lots of talking to Zoe this week and my head is spinning about what's going to happen now. I'm not talking to Mum about any of this, of course, because she'd probably make up a load of rubbish about how everything was going to be all right! What does she know?

Zoe has told me loads about her dad and his girlfriend. She really hates the girlfriend (not the same one as I was taking about the other day) and her dad sounds like a total loser. I hope my dad won't turn into one, but what if he does? He might stop wanting to see us? He has phoned every night this week, but I think that's just out of guilt, or some kind of early effort to keep in touch. What if that fades away 'til he never rings anymore? And then there's this woman that Dad's 'shacked up with,' as Zoe calls it. Will she rant on at Mum and try to stop Dad seeing us? It's scary to think about. I don't want to not see Dad anymore, even if I do hate his girlfriend and what they've done to us.

Anyway, tonight, Nat and I have packed a bag of clothes and stuff to go and stay at Dad's tomorrow. It feels so strange. Mum was acting very cheery at tea time; chatting about how it would be nice for us to stay with Dad and how he'd probably spoil us rotten: That's what Weekend-Dads are supposed to do, apparently. This was, yet again, another of Mum's fake-personas. (Yes, I like big words. I am a budding writer after all!)

Nat asked, 'Will that Eve lady be there?'

Big mistake, little sister!

'Do you mean Dad's girlfriend?' said Mum, spitting out the last word. 'I expect so. After all, it's her house he's living in.' Mum's mood changed after that. She was quiet, but when either of us asked even a simple question she snapped at us.

Charming!

We certainly didn't ask about the girlfriend any more.

I'm not sure I want to go, but Nat is kind of excited. She wants to see Dad, of course, but I think she's curious about this Eve person. So am I, but it'll be so awkward, won't it? I keep trying to imagine what she looks like and all I come up with is some sort of nasty troll-looking wicked stepmother from a fairytale. Stupid imagination!

Zoe messaged me:

> You ready to meet the wicked stepmother then?
> Mwa-hah-hah! 😁

(Honestly, she's so child-ish!)

> Me: Ooh I'm scared! I'm hoping she doesn't boil us alive in a cauldron of frog's legs and toad's eyeballs!

(Okay, I'm child-ish too!)

> Zoe: Toad's eyeballs would be very small!
> Me: ???
> Me again: Giraffe's eyeballs then!
> Zoe: No! I love giraffes!
> Me: Okay, rat's eyeballs then!
> Zoe: Better, but still small
> Me: 😛
> Zoe: LOL xxx

So, I'm saying goodnight, Diary, and hoping I live to tell the tale to you tomorrow night!

Saturday 20th January

Dearest Diary,

Nine o'clock, on the dot, Dad was ringing the doorbell.
Nat had been looking out of the window for the last
ten minutes and rushed to open the door. She yelled,
'Daaaaaaaaaad!'
'Hello my little Scatty Natty,' he grinned, bending
down to scoop her up, and giving her a big kiss. 'I've
missed you.'
(Yeah, really? I thought.)
I said hello, whilst studying my shoes.
'Hi Lou. How have you been?' He tried to kiss me. I
moved.
Stupid question, I thought. 'Okay,' I said.
Mum came up behind us.
Dad said, 'Hi,' apologetically, now looking at *his* shoes
'How are you?'
Mum chose not to answer the question, but said,
'They've got everything they'll need. I want them back
by ten tomorrow morning.'
'Right, 'said Dad. Then he turned to us and put on his
bright and breezy voice. 'Okay, let's go, girls.'
We said goodbye solemnly to Mum. She was pretending
to be very cool about it, but I did worry about her when
we were riding in Dad's car. I wondered if she cried
when we'd gone. Dad was asking us loads of questions
about school and what we'd been doing all week. He

didn't mention Mum though, so I thought it best to keep off the subject too. As we neared Queen Elizabeth Road, Dad started talking faster and faster.

'You're going to meet someone new this morning.'

Obviously, I thought!

'You'll really like her when you get to know her. I know she won't be like your mum, and she's not meant to be the same as Mum, but just give her a chance and be nice to her, eh?' Dad waffling on. She's really fun to be with and she really likes children. She's really nice.'

REALLY?

'Does she have any children?' I asked, abruptly.

'No, not yet,' Dad said. 'She's a bit younger than me.'

'Are you going to have a baby with her, Dad?' I asked, much to Dad's surprise.

'Well, we might, I don't know.'

'You'd have to get married first, wouldn't you Dad?' said Nat, as if she knew all about these things.

'No, they wouldn't,' I snapped, knowing much more about these things! 'You can have kids any time. But you're not going to, are you Dad?'

'No, no, we're not. Let's take things slowly. Just meet her and see if you like her. And please, be nice to her, okay?'

We were just pulling up outside the house. Dad looked like he might be going to faint!

I quickly messaged Zoe.

We're here...

I didn't expect a reply (Saturday morning) but one came back.

> Goodbye my BFF. I hope being boiled alive is not too painful. Mwah-hah-hah! 😁

Crazy girl!

Number 112 Queen Elizabeth Road was a small terraced house, with one window downstairs next to the door, and two windows above. I wondered if there would be enough room for us all. My stomach was doing somersaults now. All the nasty words about Zoe's dad's girlfriend burbled round in my brain. Nat was fidgety too, looking up at the house with big saucer eyes.

As Dad was getting our stuff out of the boot, Nat whispered to me, 'Do we have to stay here tonight?'

I squeezed her hand. 'It'll be alright,' I smiled, trying to convince myself as much as Nat.

Dad bent into the car. 'Ready?' he grinned.

I smiled my best plastic smile, and pushed Nat gently out of the car. 'Yep!'

As we walked through the door, I could hear music playing in the kitchen and I was surprised that it was the kind of music I listen to. The hall was quite dark and narrow.

'Hi love, we're home,' Dad shouted along the hall.

LOVE?

 HOME?

 WHOA!

That wasn't right. Before I realised I'd said anything, the words came out. 'We're not home, actually Dad. This is NOT our home.' I bit my tongue. Oops! I hadn't meant for that to happen.

But Dad apologised. 'Sorry. I meant *I'm* home. But one day I hope you'll think of this as a second home.' He has such a pathetic smile when he wants to.

I felt bad then and just a teeny bit sorry for him.

'Hi sweetheart,' came a voice from the kitchen. Then she appeared, sweeping up the passageway in a long, hippyish skirt and white flouncy top. She kissed Dad, on the lips, in front of us! (Mum never did that.) Then she said, 'Hello Natalie; Louise. It's good to meet you at last.'

Nat and I did a sort of smile. The kind where your mouth turns up a bit but your eyes don't take part. Must have learnt that from Mum. I managed a 'Hi.' Nat didn't speak.

'Let's go into the lounge,' Dad suggested, and led the way.

It was small, but light flooded in from the back window and made the room feel cosy and cheerful. That wasn't how I wanted to feel, thanks very much. The walls were painted in a gentle cream colour. There was a large black and white drawing above the fireplace, in a chunky wooden frame of a girl looking wistfully at a daisy chain she was making. On the mantelpiece were three photos: One of me, one of Nat and, in between them, one of Dad and her eating ice creams somewhere in the summer. Last summer? The summer when we'd gone to Spain and Dad had laughed and eaten ice creams with *us*? I glowered

at him. (Good word, that: GLOWERED! You have to say it with feeling.) Anyway, we sat down on the sofa. Dad stood in front of the fireplace and she sat in the armchair.

There was just a fraction of an awkward silence as they smiled at us and we waited. Dad cleared his throat, then gesturing towards her, he announced, 'Louise, Natalie, let me introduce you to... Eve.' He made it sound like he was introducing us to the queen! I expected a 'Ta-Da!'

Eve jumped up out of her seat and knelt in front of the sofa. 'I've been dying to meet you,' she said, smiling and taking a hand each in hers. Whoa! Before I could stop myself, I pulled my hand away. Her smile wobbled just a little before she jumped up as breezily as she could and said, 'Right, who'd like a drink and some cake? I've made some apple cake this morning.'

I said, 'Thanks,' trying to make up for the hand thing. (Embarrassing!)

'Won't be a tick.' She swished away to the kitchen.

Dad smiled at us, encouragingly. 'She's nice, isn't she? Once you get to know her a bit, you'll really like her.'

I nodded and fake-smiled, but deep down, I didn't intend to get to know her.

While we were politely eating apple cake (which, I admit, was good) Dad told us that he and Eve had planned a trip to the fair this afternoon. Every year a huge fairground came and parked up in the fields on the outskirts of town. We'd gone the last few years with Mum and Dad and had a great time. I wondered if Mum would mind us going without her. Dad was telling Eve how I'd thrown up on the waltzer last year. He even told her the embarrassing ghost train story from years ago, when I hid in the bottom of the car and wouldn't come out until I saw daylight. They were all laughing at that, except me. (I was probably glowering at Dad again.) Eve quickly suggested we tell some embarrassing stories about Dad instead. When Nat and I didn't volunteer any, she told us how, a few weeks ago, a little teeny weenie spider landed on Dad's face and he jumped around and screeched like a tarantula was attacking him! She said she had to rescue him, and the spider! Then she had to calm him down with a cup of tea. Dad went bright red, and for the first time, I found myself genuinely smiling. As I looked at Nat she was giggling behind her hands. My smile grew wider.

After lunch, we set off to the fair. Nat and I sat quietly in the back of the car.

'So,' Dad said, in his Mr. Jolly voice, 'This is nice, isn't it? Off to the fair. Wonder what we'll do first?'

No reply from the back.

'I bet Nat will want me to win her a coconut, eh?' He chortled like any self-respecting Mr. Jolly would do. 'Remember how awful I am at that, Nat?'

Nat nodded.

'Oh, and I'll have to have a go on the hammer thing,' he said.

Eve joined in. 'I bet he can't even get it to shoot up half way, can he girls?'

No answer from the back.

'Cheek!' said Dad, 'I once got it right to the top.'

Eve persisted. 'Do you like the dodgems?'

'I do,' Nat piped up. I frowned at her.

'What about you, Louise?'

'No.'

'Ah well, never mind. What's your favourite ride?'

'Haven't got one,' I said.

She gave up then with an, 'Oh, okay.'

HA!

Silence returned to the car.

I messaged Zoe.

Still alive.

When we arrived, we walked around together, looking at the stalls and rides. Nat and I do love the fair really and I found myself talking a bit more. Nat was getting excited and asking Dad which rides we could go on. Neither of us really spoke to Eve unless she spoke to us. Maybe I was imagining things, but people were giving us funny looks. There's no way Eve looks old enough to be our mum. She looks so young with her black, wavy hair down to her waist, pierced nose and four earrings in both ears. She's soooo different to Mum. Poor Mum. She can't help it if she's old and a bit wrinkly. Dad's not so hot himself. What does Eve even see in him?

Note to self: Tell Mum that Eve is very ugly and twice Dad's age: A bit more like that troll I had imagined. That should make Mum feel good.

We went on loads of rides and bought candy floss. We played hoopla, hook-a-duck and camel racing. Dad managed to win a coconut. I don't know how. The closest he came to hitting anything was when he knocked the

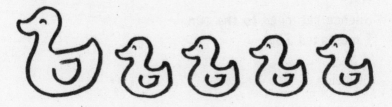

stall holder's hat off. I think she gave him the coconut to get rid of him. Eve was up for any kind of ride. Dad persuaded me to go on the Twister with her while he took Nat to the Merry-go-round. We squealed together and I couldn't help laughing as I was flung against her. When we all came back together, Nat needed to go to the loo. Dad and I were just about to go on the Sky Flyer and didn't want to lose our place in the queue, so Eve said she'd take Nat. Nat was okay about it, so they went off to the toilets and we said we'd meet at the burger stand when we'd finished the ride. It was an awesome ride. We laughed the whole time and Dad screamed louder than me!

Afterwards we walked to the burger stand to meet Nat and Eve. We waited ten minutes. 'They're taking ages!' Dad sighed, looking at his watch again. 'What on earth are they doing?'

I was wondering that myself. Nat wasn't one for hanging around when she needed a wee. 'Should we go and meet them, Dad?'

'Let's give them five more minutes. Maybe they're on their way here and we might miss them if we go wandering off.'

So, we waited but still they didn't come. I was starting to get butterflies in my stomach again and horrid thoughts started to flit across my mind. What if Eve was really a wicked stepmother and she'd just been waiting for the chance to kidnap one of us? After all, she'd said she was dying to meet us!

I looked at Dad. His forehead was wrinkling and his

mouth was all scrunched up.

'Let's go and see where they are,' he decided. We walked, rather quickly, over to the toilets. 'You go in and see if they're still there.'

They weren't. So, we walked even more quickly back to the burger van. No sign of them.

'Oh, you know what?' said Dad, feigning a smile. 'There's another burger van over the other side of the field. They've probably gone to the wrong one. I bet they're standing, wondering where we've got to. Come on.'

We marched over to the other van. They weren't there. Now it wasn't butterflies in my stomach but kangaroos, doing great thumping leaps. I felt sick. How would we break the news to Mum that Nat had been kidnapped? Dad started rubbing his eyebrow like he always did when he was worried or thinking hard.

'What do you think has happened, Dad?' I asked tentatively, not really wanting him to confirm my fears.

'Oh, they're probably wandering round the fairground looking for us, just like we're looking for them. Come on, all we can do is keep searching.'

'Why don't you call her, Dad?

Dad got out his phone and up came a picture of her: The wicked stepmother, disguised as an ordinary woman!

'Sorry, this is spoiling your fun,' he said to me whilst

touching the screen to call her.

Spoiling my fun! Is that what he thought I was thinking? 'Dad, I'm not bothered about my fun, I'm just worried about Nat.'

Yes, sorry love, of course. So am I, but I'm sure she's safe with Eve. They're just a bit lost, that's all.'

Her phone went to answerphone. Dad left a message. Why wasn't she answering?

I messaged Zoe.

M: She's kidnapped Nat!!!
Zoe : Zipes! 😳

(Another of Zoe's stupid words!)

Me: What am I gonna do?
Zoe: Call the cops??

(Cops? What has she been watching?)

So, I said, 'Dad, we should call the police!'

Just then, we saw Eve walking over by the hoop-la, but she was alone. What had she done with Nat? Then I thought, why would she still be here if she had taken Nat? I was relieved and terrified all at once. Relieved that she couldn't have kidnapped Nat, but terrified that Nat must be out there somewhere by herself.

'Dad, there's Eve!' I yelled. We ran towards her, both shouting her name.

She was almost crying and gasping for breath, like she'd been running. 'Oh Mike, it's Nat, she's lost. I'm so sorry. I've been looking everywhere for her and for you. I've been round the whole field twice and I can't see her anywhere. I'm so sorry. I'm sorry.' She burst into tears and flung herself at Dad.

Dad grabbed her by the arms and held her away from him, so he could look into her face.

He told her to calm down. 'Where did you last see her?'

She gulped and tried to compose herself. 'She was in the toilets. I let her go in by herself, she wanted to, and I waited outside. Then I saw this sweet stall and thought it would be nice to get the girls some sweets, so I shouted into the toilets to say where I was going and I'd be back in a minute. When I came back she was gone. I looked in every cubicle, everywhere. She'd gone. I'm so stupid, I'm sorry.' She started to blub again.

'Too right!' I burst out, 'How stupid is that to leave a little kid alone at a fairground.' I sounded just like Mum. 'I shouldn't have let her go off with YOU! We don't even know you!'

Dad had a go at me in a sort of mind-your-manners kind of voice. 'Louise!'

I just shouted at him. I didn't care. 'What? It's all your fault. Nat has probably been abducted and it's all because you've gone off with her!'

'Enough!' Dad shouted. 'Now let's all calm down. We'll only find her if we think clearly and work together.

Is there an information point or something here? We could see if they could make an announcement. Where else would she have gone?'

Eve suggested we split up and meet in half an hour back here.

But I didn't want her finding Nat when she was frightened and all alone. 'Dad, you can't trust her.' All my frightening thoughts were about to pour out of my mouth. Eve looked horrified and about to cry again.

'You're not helping, Lou. I think that would be a good idea to split up,' he said. 'We'll meet you back here in half an hour, okay?'

Eve nodded, biting her lip, and hurried away. Dad and I went in the opposite direction. We searched everywhere we could think of. We didn't see an information point. There were so many people, it was hopeless. Dad was frantically asking people if they'd seen Nat, describing her to them: Small, shoulder-length brown hair, freckles, brown eyes, red jumper and jeans. People shook their heads and promised to keep an eye out for her. Half an hour didn't seem long enough, but Dad said we should go back to meet Eve. She was alone. Dad was trying to keep calm, but he was not doing a very good job. My mind was going crazy.

'I think I'd better call the police. I don't know what else to do. She's been missing for nearly an hour.' He got his phone out again and called 999. He was describing Nat and telling them how long she'd been gone. The police asked him for his car registration and said they'd send someone to meet us at our car.

Dad said he'd go there straight away. Eve asked if we should keep looking. Dad said good idea. We should go round the fairground one more time and meet back at the car. He meant me to go with her. If he thought I was going with her, he was wrong.

'I'm coming with you Dad.'

'Oh. Okay, Lou.' I saw him shoot an apologetic glance at Eve. After what she'd done! I shot her a dramatic accusing stare! Dad and I hurried off towards the car.

'Do you think Nat could have been abducted, Dad?' I asked.

He stopped abruptly and, as I looked into his face, I knew he did. 'Oh Lou, this is such a nightmare. I'm sure she's just wandering round the fairground, but we have to act quickly because... you never know what kind of people are about.'

We began walking again, quicker than before. 'Are you going to phone Mum?'

'No... not yet. Don't want to worry her right now. I'm sure we'll find Nat. We'll just give it a bit more time. Wait 'til the police arrive.' He was scared of Mum and stalling for time.

I felt sorry for him (a bit). But if he hadn't left Mum none of this would have happened. Mum would have been at the fair with us, and she would never have left Nat alone in the toilets. I was really angry with him. As we marched along I wanted to give him a kick in the shins. I didn't though. (I decided to tell you about it instead, Dear Diary.)

However, as we came in sight of the car, joy and

relief whooshed through me. Dad had seen her too.

'Natalie!' we both screamed and sprinted towards the car. She was sitting on the grass at the back of the car, with her knees tucked up to her chin. When she saw us, she jumped up and started running towards us. We fell on each other in a big heap.

'Nat, oh Nat, thank goodness you're safe,' Dad gasped, almost crying.

She clung to him.

'It's okay darling. It's okay. We're here now. We're all together. You're safe.'

'It's alright Nat, we won't let you get lost ever again,' I added.

When she'd calmed down a little, Dad picked her up and put her in the passenger seat of the car. He draped his coat over her like you see people do in movies.

'What happened love, and how did you get back here?'

'Well, Eve was gone when I came out of the toilet so I didn't know what to do.'

I interrupted. 'She said she'd told you where she was going.'

'She didn't,' said Nat.

'I knew she was lying,' I hissed. Zoe's wicked stepmother image burst into my head, like a scene from a Disney movie.

'Maybe you didn't hear her, darling. She said she shouted in to you,' suggested Dad.

'She didn't... Well I didn't hear her, it was noisy.'

'So, what did you do?' Dad prompted.

'I thought I'd come and find you, and I couldn't, so I

walked around looking for you and I still couldn't find you.'

'Didn't anyone stop you and ask where your Mummy and Daddy were?' asked Dad.

'A man did, but I said I wasn't with my Mummy and Daddy, just my Daddy, and he wanted me to go with him to find you, but I said I didn't go with strangers and I ran off.'

'That was very sensible, wasn't it Dad?' I said, patting Nat on the shoulder.

'Definitely. Then what did you do?'

'I cried a bit, behind a van, because I was frightened.'

'I know, sweetheart, but you were very brave really. How did you get to the car?'

'Well I remembered on a cartoon once, this little boy got lost and his Mum had told him if he got lost to go back to the car and wait, so I did that. I had to look really hard to find our car, but I saw Poops in the back, so I knew this was ours.'

Dad smiled and hugged Nat tight. 'Hooray for Poops! You are an amazing girl.'

'Yeah, well done Nat, I don't think I would have thought of that,' I said.

Dad phoned the police to tell them she'd been found and they recalled the police car they were sending. 'Right, we'll just wait for Eve, then we'll go back home. She'll be so relieved to see you. She was frantic. She'd gone to get you some sweets. Not a great idea, but she was just trying to be nice. So please, Louise, don't give her a hard time.'

I just made a humpfing noise and shrugged my shoulders.

'She shouldn't have left me, Daddy. Mummy will be cross,' Nat said.

Dad frowned. 'You're right, love, she shouldn't, and Mummy will be cross.'

'Are you going to tell her?' I asked.

'Of course, I am. She'd find out from you two if I didn't, and then she'd never let it drop.' Then he mumbled, 'She probably won't anyway!'

At that point, Eve came rushing over. She'd seen the three of us by the car, so she was full of, 'Oh Natalie, thank God you're safe, I'm so relieved. I'm so sorry' etc. What a load of gushing garbage! How could she care about us when she doesn't even know us?

Nat said, 'It's okay, you made a mistake, but I'm okay now.'

'That's very sweet of you, Natalie. You're a lovely little girl.' Eve bent into the car and hugged Nat.

I couldn't help smirking to myself as Nat added, 'My Mummy is going to be ever so cross though.'

Eve bit her lip and glanced at Dad.

'Yes, well, we'll face that one tomorrow,' Dad said. 'Right, let's go. I'm looking forward to a nice quiet evening in front of some mindless Saturday night TV.'

We got into the car and drove back to Dad's. Nat was quiet all the way there. Now and again she let out a little sob, like she was still calming down. I tried to make her laugh with Poops, but she just snatched him from me and cuddled him. Fair enough! She'd had a traumatic day.

I messaged Zoe:

She's found
Zoe: Alive?
Me: Yes, alive, you idiot!
Zoe: EPIC
Me. IKR
Zoe: Wicked Stepmother hasn't struck yet then? 😕

I didn't reply. At that moment, I didn't feel like making a joke of it all. It had been a bit too close to disaster for my liking. I put my phone on silent and flung it in my bag. I'd deal with the hundreds of messages I knew Zoe was about to send me, later.

When we arrived at the front door, that was the final straw. Nat burst into tears. 'I want to go home,' she wailed. 'I want Mummy. I don't want to stay here.'

Dad and Eve tried to calm her down but nothing would persuade her to stay. They did manage to coax her into the house to have some tea, but only because Dad promised to take us straight home afterwards.

As we got into the car to go home, Eve apologised again. 'I'm so sorry, girls. This has been an awful day for you. I'll make it up to you. Next time will be great, I promise.' She waved as we drove off. I deliberately ignored her and Nat wasn't looking.

Next time? I didn't see there being a next time if

Mum had anything to do with it.

*

I was right.

'Next time!' she screeched at Dad, as he tried to explain and apologise again. 'You don't think for one minute that that woman is going to be left in charge of my girls again, do you?'

'She wasn't left in charge,' Dad protested.

'Exactly right! You were supposed to be looking after them. You! Their father. Anything could have happened, anything!' she screamed at him. Mum was bright red in the face.

'But it didn't, Linda! Children get lost all the time. Remember when you lost Lou at the seaside when she was only eighteen months?'

Nat and I sat quietly on the sofa, watching them shout at each other. We'd never seen Mum and Dad go for each other like this before.

'It was only five minutes, and I thought you had taken her to the shop,' Mum snarled.

'Yes, well, everything's my fault in the end, isn't it? You never take the blame,' Dad growled.

'Only because it usually is your fault! Anyway, your girlfriend's got no idea how to look after children, that's obvious. I can't trust her, or you!'

Dad slumped down into a chair. He leant forward, resting his elbows on his knees, and sank his head into his hands. No one spoke for ages. Mum stared at him, waiting for him to take his turn in the slanging match.

But he didn't say anything. Nat cuddled in to me and Poops. I couldn't move. Then slowly, Dad looked up.

'What – a – mess,' he said, each word preceded by a pause. Mum didn't start ranting again. She waited for him to have another turn. 'I'm sorry. I don't know what else to say.' There was a long pause. I tried to think of something to say to fill it, but I couldn't. Nat's eyes darted from Mum to Dad and she kept squeezing my arm. Then Dad said, 'Do you want me to come back home?'

Nat and I looked at each other. Dad was going to come back! He was going to leave Evil Eve and come home where he belonged!

But then Mum spoilt it. She started ranting again. 'Oh yes, that would be just great! You'd come back here and be miserable. All you'd think about was that woman, all the time. Then you'd start seeing her again and nothing would change. What do you think that would do to the girls? No way, Mike. The damage is done. I don't want you back. I want to start rebuilding our lives. I couldn't possibly just start all over again after what you've done. I want a divorce and I mean to start the process off immediately.'

Nat and I were right there and yet they were carrying on as if we were invisible. Nat's face crumpled, she began to cry and ran out of the room.

'Well thank you very much!' I shouted, and stormed after her.

Both Mum and Dad were stunned, because they stood very still, saying nothing. I found Nat in her bedroom, sobbing into her pillow.

'Come here.' I held her.

'I hate them! I hate them both!' she cried.

'I know. They're stupid, selfish idiots! They've ruined everything!' I said.

*

The next thing we heard was the front door closing and Dad's car driving away.

Mum came up.

'GO AWAY!' I yelled at her.

She came closer, her arms outstretched towards us. She tried to cuddle Nat, but Nat pushed her away and clung to me.

'Leave us alone Mum,' I said, quietly.

So, she did. She went to her room and I could hear her crying.

So, here I am. Nat is asleep and I am in my normal bed, not at Dad's new house, thank goodness.

Today was rubbish! Dad's girlfriend, Evil Eve, as I'm now calling her, is an idiot. Dad thinks she's so cool and he never even got angry with her about losing Nat. He got angry with me for being annoyed with her! And she's so young anyway. And she's got her nose pierced. Dad would go ape if I did that! It's disgusting, him going off with her. He's too old! Then tonight he offers to come back home and Mum tells him, no

45

way! What is Mum on? Everything could be back to normal, well sort of. But no, she's too selfish as well. Too proud to take him back. They just don't think about us!

Right now, *I* feel like leaving!!

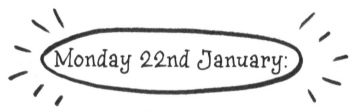

Monday 22nd January:

Dear Diary,

The Plot Thickens! **Dun-dun-duh!**

As soon as I arrived at school today, Zoe wanted to know all about what had happened. She was a bit miffed with me for not messaging her yesterday and just cutting her off on Saturday, but I couldn't be bothered with anyone yesterday, not even you, Dear Diary.

Zoe got well into the fairground story and her theory was that my Dad had blown it big time. 'My mum would have had a meltdown!' she said. 'And that Evil Eve woman sounds totally bzonkers, if you ask me. I mean, what person in their right mind would leave a little kid alone in the loo at the fair! Any nutter could be lurking in there!'

'I know,' I agreed. 'She tried to be all matey with us, but that was just a front. I think she's trying to scare us off so we don't want to go and see Dad anymore.'

'Or it could be that she's trying to make your mum so mad that she won't let you go,' suggested Zoe. 'So your mum looks like the bad guy.'

That made sense. Yesterday, Mum had banned us from going to Dad's house. She said that he could see us on a Saturday, but under no circumstances could he take us back to their house or let Eve have any contact with us. I was in my bedroom and she was next door in hers.

I heard her snarling down the phone at him. I could tell Dad was saying things about being reasonable, when Mum shrieked, 'need to build a good relationship for the future? That's rich!' Then she roared, like a lion (not kidding!) and I heard the phone being thrown across the room. I didn't realise my mum had a temper like that.

'Evil Eve wants your dad all to herself,' Zoe said. 'And if she can make it seem like your mum is the bad guy, then she's the winner. Your dad'll get fed up with only seeing you for day visits and not being able to bring Evil Eve. The visits will get less and less. You'll have to get back in there and stop her from getting her evil claws all the way in, if you want to keep seeing your dad. Or maybe he's not worth it.' She shrugged. Clearly her dad wasn't worth fighting for.

Zoe may be a bit crazy, but she's often right about stuff like that, Dear Diary. I've been mulling it over all day. Mum was acting like the bad guy, but maybe it was just what Evil Eve had planned. I have to find a way to persuade Mum to let us go back to Dad's. I can't let that woman win and get my dad all to herself! Not sure how to persuade Mum, at the moment though. Any ideas, Diary?

Saturday 27th January

Dear Diary,

I'm so glad I have you to splurge this all out to. Who else would want to listen to it all? You're so understanding.

We went out for a 'day visit' with Dad today. Sounds totally rubbish, doesn't it? Like being allowed out of prison for the day for good behaviour. It felt so false and unreal, like we were just killing time 'til 4 o'clock when Mum had told him he had to bring us back. He didn't argue because he's trying to be on his best behaviour, to see if that might change her mind. Good luck there, Dad!

We trailed round town and he bought us a few things. Nat was really pleased with her new cuddly dog. She has a collection of at least a hundred now. She adores dogs, but Mum and Dad would never let us have one. They said they're too much trouble. Hmmmm!

I was bored. I would rather have been at home, listening to my music and chatting to my friends. And I had homework to do, which meant I would have to spend half of tomorrow doing that instead of going out. Dad was trying to be Mister Jolly, but honestly, he was just being Mister Annoying! At least Nat enjoyed it, I think. He didn't talk about Evil Eve or the fairground incident, thank goodness.

He took us to the cinema in the afternoon. At least I

was pleased about that, because it
had been drizzling all morning and
we were getting soaked. We had to
see something that was suitable for
Nat, but that was okay. As I have
previously admitted to you, Dear
Diary, I don't have an aversion to a bit of kids' stuff
now and again. When the movie finished, it was nearly
four. I was thinking Dad would be in trouble with Mum.

Blah
Blah
Blah

*

We were going to be late by about ten minutes. Oh
great, Dad! Just give Mum more ammunition against
you! In the car, Dad told us he wanted to discuss some
things with Mum. Brilliant!

Of course, her face was like a brewing storm when
she opened the door. 'I said home by four!'

'I know. I'm sorry. The film ran over,' Dad said.

She muttered as we walked past her and was about to
shut the door on Dad, as he said, 'Can I have a word?'
She hesitated, so he said, 'It's important.' I thought she
was still going to say no, but she let him in.

I took Nat into the living room and turned the TV on,
loud, in case of more shouting. Then, I peered round
the door to see them disappearing into the kitchen.
I crept into the hallway to listen, in case they said
anything I needed to hear.

Dad was saying, 'The divorce will be held up you know,
Linda, if you make it difficult for Eve and I to have
the girls regularly.'

DIVORCE!

Yes, my dearest Diary. He mentioned the dreaded D word! When had that been decided? No one had talked to me or Nat about it.

'What do you expect me to do, Mike? I can't trust the woman. The first time they go to your house she nearly loses my daughter. She's irresponsible, you can't deny it.'

'It was an accident. For goodness sake, can't you let it drop? Give her the chance to prove to you that she can look after the girls perfectly well. She's not forgiven herself for what happened and she just wants to put things right.'

'Maybe that's what you want, but I'm not so sure it's what she really wants. She's young and arty, from what I gather, so I can't think she'd want two kids spoiling your cosy little love nest!'

Mum was getting worked up. And, she must have been looking at my diary, because I'd told her Eve was about fifty and ugly!

Dad started raising his voice now. 'You don't know what you're talking about! She's intelligent and caring and she likes the girls. She wants them in our lives.' Then there was a short pause and Dad's voice became calmer again. 'Look, she says she'd like to come and talk to you. She wants you to hear from her own lips how sorry she is and to ask for a second chance.'

Mum laughed, but it was more of a cackle. 'No way! I'm not letting her into my house. I never want to set eyes on her. And she's not having access to the girls.

She's crazy and incompetent!'

Dad shouted, 'You're the crazy one! She's making an effort and you won't even let her try.'

'I just want my girls to be safe!' Mum shouted back.

'No! You just can't stand to see me happy, and you can't stand the thought that the girls might like her. After all, one day, she will be their stepmother, whether you like it or not, and you can't stop her seeing them forever.'

'Ha! Their stepmother?' Mum was screeching by now. 'Their wicked stepmother, more like. She's already tried to lose one of them! And I can stop her seeing them, you just watch me!'

'I've had enough of this!'

That was my cue to retreat hastily into the living room. Dad stormed out of the kitchen, slamming the front door as he left.

I sat on the sofa, staring at the TV. Great! My parents were getting a divorce. My eyes started to fill up. Nat was laughing at some stupid TV show. How was this meant to be funny? I could feel myself starting to fume. And then I remembered something which made me even angrier.

I stormed into the kitchen where Mum was sitting at the table.

'Mum, have you been reading my diary?' I stood, arms folded across my chest.

She looked up, clutching a tissue. Her eyes were red. 'What?' she said, as if she hadn't understood a simple question.

'Have you been reading my diary?' I asked again. 'It's just that you seem to know a lot about what Eve looks like, when I told you she was old and ugly.'

Mum groaned. 'Oh, you heard us. We were being loud, weren't we? Did Natalie hear?'

'No, she's mesmerised by some stupid game show on TV. Have you though, Mum?' She still hadn't answered my question.

'What? Your diary? No love. I didn't even realise you kept a diary.'

'Well how did you know what Eve looks like, then?'

She smiled. 'Oh, come on, Lou. You were so over the top when you described her, that I guessed you were telling me the opposite of what she was really like. I was young and quite pretty once myself, you know.'

She smiled so feebly then, that my heart did this big lurch and the anger was defeated. 'You still are Mum, pretty I mean; not young, obviously.'

She suddenly burst out laughing. Then she came over and hugged me. I realised what I'd just said and I started laughing too.

'Oops! Sorry Mum.' We sat down again. 'Do you really think Eve's wicked and crazy?'

'My, my, you were listening carefully, weren't you? Oh, I don't know. I'm just worried, that's all, about lots of things.'

'Are you really going to go through with the divorce?' I asked.

She raised her eyebrows. 'Yes, Lou, we are. I can't see any way back now.' We sat in silence for a while.

'Yeah, I think you're right,' I mused. 'I guess I knew he wouldn't be coming back, deep down. I think maybe we should give Eve a chance; try and keep the peace.'

'You do?' She sounded surprised. 'Good grief! Listen to us. We sound like best friends, having a coffee and sharing our problems. Only, you're the one with all the advice.'

When I came up to my room, I messaged Zoe.

Me: Mum and Dad are using the D word ☹
Zoe: SMH
Me: IKR
Zoe: I'm here for ya
Me. I know. Thanks BFF
Zoe: ☺

*

Earlier this evening, I heard Mum actually apologise to Dad on the phone! I admire her for that. It takes guts. She said she'd think about us being allowed to go over to his house again.

Yay!

I think!

Dear Diary,

Zoe said my mum was soft to give in so easily. We were walking back from school this afternoon and I told her what Mum had said about Eve becoming our wicked stepmother. Zoe laughed, then in her most dramatic actory voice, (which she loves to use, especially if lots of people are around) she said, 'Maybe your mum's right! Maybe Evil Eve is the wicked stepmother in Babes in the Wood, who tries to lose the children. Or maybe she's Cinderella's wicked stepmother and will make you slaves in her house, doing all the chores. Or worse still, maybe she'll try to kill you, like Snow White! Mwah hah hah!' She cackled like an evil witch, very loudly, right in my ear. Other kids were pointing and laughing at us from the other side of the road.

'Shut up, you idiot!' I gave her a shove, but then we giggled together all the way home. She came to my house for tea and kept cackling quietly in my ear while we were eating. Mum was giving her funny looks and I kept kicking her under the table.

'What's wrong with Zoe?' Nat whispered, behind her hand, thinking Zoe wouldn't notice. Of course, she did notice, so did a cackle in Nat's face.

I said, 'She's just TOTALLY MAD!'

Nat looked a bit startled, but she was used to Zoe's antics.

Zoe doesn't mind being called that, in fact, she takes it as a compliment, because she likes being quirky. One day, I reckon she'll be an actress. She just loves an audience! After tea, we went to my room to listen to music. Zoe started prancing round the bedroom with my hairbrush, singing at the top of her voice, like a total diva. She stood in front of my full-length mirror, totally going over the top and being crazy. I was rolling on the bed, killing myself laughing at her. Then she dragged me off the bed and made me join in. So, I grabbed a can of deodorant and started wiggling my bum around and pretending to sing; with passion!

I sometimes wish I could be more like Zoe. She never seems to let anything worry her. She's full of confidence. When people at school laugh at her daft antics, she just shrugs and laughs along with them. When her mum and Rick have blazing rows, she laughs it off and just calls them something obnoxious (love that word). I love Zoe, she makes me feel fab and I can forget about all the rubbish stuff for a while.

Mum was patient with us for ages before she finally came knocking on the bedroom door and told us to pipe down a bit. She did have a big grin on her face though. She likes Zoe.

Zoe wanted me to go into town with her on Saturday and I'd really like to, but Mum has agreed that we can give it another try with Dad, so we're going back to his and Evil Eve's house. I'd better do it, since it was my idea to try and make things work. I'm kind of glad, but also not looking forward to it. Just don't know what to make of her. I suppose I've only met her once and that didn't go so well. I know I told Mum about keeping the peace and all that, but it's just awkward. Don't know what to say to her. I won't be too nice because that's like being disloyal to Mum, but on the other hand I need to be a bit nice for Dad's sake.

Aaaaaaggh!

And I'd better stop calling her Evil Eve. It could be embarrassing if that slipped out!

Saturday 3rd February:

My Dear Diary,

It's been a bit of a boring week at school. Not much to report. Sorry to keep you waiting for the next instalment of the story of my life. But here it is.

Today is the day I've been looking forward to and dreading at the same time, all week. Dad came to pick us up and did his best grovelling to Mum. Mum took full advantage of it, making sure Dad knew exactly what she expected of him: Phone her every few hours and have us back by nine that evening (no staying over). Even though Nat had been excited all week about seeing Dad, she was a bit nervous now it came to actually going, and even asked if Mum could come, saying that we could all have a nice day out together. (I know she's much younger than me, but really???) Dad managed to persuade her (with Mum's help, which surprised me) that she would be okay without Mum. So, we set off. My stomach was churning as I recalled how I'd felt about Eve when we last saw her. Some of the things I'd said were coming back to haunt me.

Dad was Mr. Jolly in the car. I sat in the back with Nat and he kept looking in the mirror and making her giggle with silly faces and putting on silly voices. He's such an idiot, but he is kind of funny. He's like a big kid when he's excited.

As we pulled up to the house, Eve was at the door.

She had a big grin on her face like she was over the moon to see us. She waved enthusiastically as the car stopped. I looked down into my lap. What was I supposed to do? Nat waved back, but also gripped my hand. We stepped out of the car and Eve came towards us as if she was going to hug us. At the last minute, she thought better of it. Phew! I don't know what I might have done if she'd tried it.

Instead, she put on a chirpy voice (literally reminded me of a little bird; kind of high pitched and tweety). 'Hi girls. It's great to see you again. Come inside. I've been making loads of sweet treats that are probably really bad for your teeth!' She laughed.

'Babes in the Wood!' warned Zoe's voice in my head. I could hear her breaking into 'Mwah hah hah!'

It felt a bit awkward with Eve at first. No one mentioned the fairground fiasco. She was very nice to us and I really tried to be nice back. I kept thinking of what I'd said to Mum. Dad asked us if we wanted to go out but we didn't really want to after last time. I suggested watching a movie. Eve made us hot chocolate with marshmallows and cream. (We never get that at home, only for a special treat if we're out in a café). Dad and Eve let Nat and I choose the film and I let Nat choose, so we ended up watching one of her favourite Disney films: Frozen. I thought it would be very tedious (I must have seen it fifty million times!) but I just said to myself, 'No, I'm being Nice-Louise today' and put up with it, in the interests of family harmony. But, it turned out to be quite a laugh because we all joined in the songs. Not sure how Eve knew them, since she doesn't have children, but she seemed to know some of the words better than me and Nat. Dad kept putting on his various singing voices: Opera-singer voice to blast out the powerful 'Let it Go!' (on his knees in the middle of the room, arms outstretched, eyes closed!!!) and then his squeaky American-kid voice for 'Do you wanna build a snowman?' Eve was equally as silly, and before long Nat was relaxed and laughing hysterically at both of them. Totally embarrassing if you ask me, but hey, it was fun too. I messaged Zoe:

Going well so far

She didn't get back straight away, but it wasn't too long before my phone pinged.

Zoe: What u up to?
Me: Dad being crazy. Eve not so bad
Zoe: Evil Eve, u mean...
Me: Trying not to think of her as that. It might slip out
Zoe: Ooh don't forget what she did last time? Maybe she's got u under her spell...
Me: SMH Whatevs
Zoe: U being cool?
Me: 😐
Zoe: Just be careful... Remember Snow White Stepmother

– disguise – poisoned apple - DEAD!
Me: Drama Queen!
Zoe: LOL x
Me: ☺

We ate pizza for lunch with home-made choc-chip muffins to follow, and loads of coke. After that, Dad insisted that we play board games. So out came his favourite game: Pictionary. My dad's drawing is awful! We were on a team together against Nat and Eve. I thought Nat would want to be on Dad's team but she was totally besotted with Eve by now. She seemed to have totally forgotten that Eve had left her alone at the fairground. Zoe's words were ringing in my head a bit, but I swished them aside and concentrated on the game.

When Dad and Eve had gone to the kitchen, laughing about something, I whispered to Nat, 'Don't you remember what she did last time?'

'Who?' asked Nat.

'Eve, of course, Dummy! At the fair.'

'When I got lost, you mean?'

'Yes.'

'I remember, but it doesn't matter. It wasn't really her fault. Anyway, I like her. She's fun. And Dad likes her. She makes him laugh a lot.' I screwed up my face, but Nat had made a good point. It had been a long time since I'd seen Dad laugh like that.

We ate loads of sweets as we played

61

and it all got very loud and silly. Yes, Dear Diary, I admit,
I was having a good time. The whole day was going well.
There were no disasters and Dad phoned Mum a few
times, as instructed. At tea-time, we had shepherd's pie
and Eve had made a trifle. I felt absolutely stuffed.

Hadn't eaten this much since Christmas! Later, Dad
said we should run off some energy, so we kicked a
football around in Jubilee Park, even though it was
getting dark. Eve and Nat versus Dad and me. They
won 2-1 and Eve ran around the field with Nat on her
back, singing 'We are the champions!' Maybe Eve isn't
too bad after all. Maybe all Zoe's cackling has just
made me more nervous.

When we were getting ready to leave, Eve asked me
if I'd had a good day.

I hesitated. 'Yeah. It's been... okay.'

'That's good. I was so nervous about you coming. You
were so mad with me last time and I don't blame you.
I'd really like us to be friends.'

I kind of smiled and said, 'Today was good. Thanks.'
I'm not sure about being friends, though.

As the car pulled away, Nat wound down the window,
shouting 'Bye!' and waving wildly.

'See you soon. Bye!' Eve shouted, waving just as
crazily back.

'You seemed to enjoy yourselves,' Dad said, looking at us in the mirror, as he drove us home.

'Yeah, it was okay.'

'I loved it,' Nat said.

Dad started humming 'Do you wanna build a Snowman!' So, I knew how he was feeling.

I messaged Zoe:

Ha! Still alive!
Zoe: Lucky escape!
Me: ☺
Zoe: LOL x

When we got home, Mum opened the door to greet us. 'Hi. Glad you're...' was all she managed to say before Nat puked all over her.

That was it! Mum went mad! 'What the...? Come on darling, let's get you inside.' She spoke through gritted teeth, shooting daggers at Dad.

'I'll speak to you in the morning,' she snarled at him. 'I can't deal with you now!'

I was just standing there, staring at the sick. 'Get in, Louise!' Mum shouted.

Before Dad could speak, she'd pulled me in and slammed the door with her foot, leaving all that disgusting sick (and Dad) on the doorstep. Nat had eaten far too much sweet stuff, of course, and then all that racing around. Mum put Nat to bed while I dithered about. Then I did a really brave thing. I got a bucket, water, disposable gloves and Dettol from under the sink and (yes, that's right, Dear Diary) I cleaned up the sick, in the interest of family harmony. (Eugh! *Sooooo* terrible, makes me gag just talking about it again.) The rubbish thing is that Mum didn't even notice, even though I left the bucket and Dettol out deliberately. (I had cleaned the bucket out though). And you can smell Dettol a mile away; it stinks nearly as bad as the sick!

Oh well. (Big sigh.)

After Mum had settled Nat in bed for the night, I tried to explain and even stick up for Dad and Eve a bit. But Mum wasn't listening.

'What was that mad woman thinking? First, she tries to lose Nat, then she tries to poison her!'

Snow White! warned Zoe in my head.

'Shut up!' I hissed.

'What?' said Mum.

I must have hissed out loud. 'Oh... mucked up, I was saying, she mucked up. Eve, I mean!'

'She certainly did!' agreed Mum, forcefully. 'Well he can forget about you going there again.'

'But Mum, she didn't do it on purpose,' I heard myself say in Eve's defence.

'Whatever! She's blown it! She wouldn't know how to look after children if... if supernanny were coming to tea!'

Mum was in a right mood, and just being ridiculous, so I came to bed to talk to someone calm and sensible: You, Dear Diary.

She's being so over the top. Honestly, they're all doing

my head in. I had a good time with Dad and Eve today. I do want to give it a go with Eve. Nat was right. Dad is happy with her. I didn't realise 'til now how little he used to laugh and stuff at home. He's changed; sort of lightened up. I'm going to have to work on Mum to get her to let us go back again. She can't stop us seeing him.

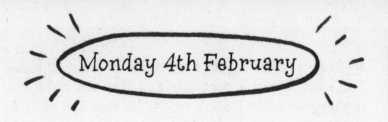

Monday 4th February

Sometimes I could really fall out with Zoe! Sorry, Dear Diary, but I just have to have a rant!

Nat stayed off school today. She was fine really, but I reckon Mum just wanted to make it seem worse when she picked up the phone to have a go at Dad. When I got to school Zoe asked me about the weekend. She couldn't stop laughing as I was telling her.

'It's not that funny Zo.' I was not in the mood!

'It is though. It's hilarious. You could make it into a Sitcom about a crazy family. We'd have to make the characters really over the top. You could be the main character. You could be the cool one who's really embarrassed by the rest of them. Your dad could be this bungling kind of idiot who keeps messing things up, your mum could be this wild woman type of character... and your sister could just keep throwing up everywhere!'

'Not even slightly funny,' I said. But she was on a roll, her mad imagination going crazy. She didn't even hear what I said. She just went on and on about her Sitcom idea. At break-time she was still doing it and Meg and Alice joined in.

I ended up storming off and they all thought I was just being sulky, so they avoided me for the rest of the day. I didn't care. In fact, I was glad. I'd had enough of them and just wanted to be on my own. Zoe can be so stupid sometimes! Surely, she could see that I was upset.

Anyway, she messaged me tonight after school.

Zoe: U K?

I hesitated. Did I want to speak to her?

Me: No! 😣
Zoe: Sorry 😵
Me: 🙁
Zoe: I made it worse, didn't I?
Me: NMH
Zoe: Stupid big mouth me!
Me: Never mind. sKK
Zoe: Still my BFF?
ME: Yep
Zoe: 😛
Me: 😎
Zoe: 🙂 😄 😛
Me: 😛

We went on a bit with silly emojis so I won't bore you with that, Diary. At least we've made up now. Feels a bit better. Mum and Dad are falling out and there's no one to talk to here, (apart from you, my lovely Diary) so I can't be doing without my BFF.

My Dear Diary,

I must apologise for not having written to you for a few weeks. Life has been mad, bad and ordinary. Mum and Dad have been arguing and Nat and I have been fed up, because we still haven't been back to Dad's since the puking incident. We have seen Dad, but on his own and usually just for a few hours on a week night and on a Saturday afternoon. Mum is digging her heels in about it and won't listen to Dad at all. So, he's been getting mad and ranting down the phone. I hear her ranting back, so I know they're both at it.

They both went to something called mediation last week. I looked it up on my phone and it said (and I quote) 'family mediation helps you resolve conflict and reach agreement on all issues surrounding separation, divorce or dissolution of civil partnership.' Well, that's good, I thought. However, as yet I haven't noticed any difference. They don't talk to me about any of it. I mean, I can understand them not talking to Nat, as she's so young, but I am old enough to be included and hear what's going on. I'm going to ask Mum about it this week.

School has just been the usual boring stuff. Homework, lessons to fall asleep in and all that.

Zoe and the girls have been good fun though. In fact, we had a sleepover at Meg's house last night. It was so cool. Meg's mum is sooooo nice. She buys us popcorn and crisps and chocolate and lets us stay up really late in Meg's bedroom, watching movies on her SUPERBIG telly.

Meg has a fab room in the attic of her house. It's really big and she's got fairy lights everywhere. AND... when we turn out all the lights, she has luminous stars all over her ceiling. It's like you're camping under the real sky.

Sooooo cool!

We watched Dirty Dancing first. Meg's older sister, Carrie, loves it. Meg sneaked it off her shelf. It's this really old movie from when our mums were teenagers, and it's all about this girl, called Baby (stupid name, if you ask me) who falls in love with this dance instructor, called Johnny (who is quite hot for a guy of my mum's generation). It's at a holiday camp. My mum would freak if she knew I was watching some of the stuff in it, (like S-E-X) but that's the beauty of a sleepover.

So, after that we got Meg's make-up out and did each other's nails and made each other up. That was so funny because we went completely crazy with the colours and everything. We actually looked like drag queens when we'd finished. We took loads of selfies and put them on Snapchat. Then we watched another movie. This time we went totally the other way and watched a Disney film. We had a vote on which one, out of Tangled, Finding Dory, Lion King and Up. Tangled won. I love that film. Rapunzel is so like,' Yeah go get 'em girl!' And I love the bit where they let off all the lanterns. It's so pretty!

I know it's a bit naff to still like Disney at my age, but you won't tell anyone, will you Diary? Anyway, all the others liked it too. Zoe asked me if Evil Eve (she still calls her that) is like the nasty witch stepmother in Tangled. Ha ha, very funny, I said. Bit bored of Zoe's wicked stepmother jokes now. Anyway, she's not my stepmother, (technically) and I haven't seen her for ages cos of Mum. I told Zoe to pack it in and stuffed some popcorn in her mouth to shut her up. She spewed it right across Meg's bed, so a popcorn fight started. Then, Meg's mum texted her to tell us to keep the noise down, so we stopped and watched the rest of the film.

After that, it was really late, so we snuggled down in loads of duvets on our airbeds (except Meg, who was in her own comfy bed) and talked in whispers to each other. It was good with the stars overhead. It felt like we were in some American movie, camping out in the

hills of Dakota (the hills of where???) and sharing secrets. But we were sworn not to tell anyone else. Do you count, Dear Diary? Erm... let me think about that? No, of course you don't! You are the best keeper of secrets.

Meg fancies this boy at school called Will Duggan. He is HOT and in year nine, but he'd never look at any of us because we're younger and he hangs around with the 'populars,' and we don't qualify. Then, Zoe told us her secret. She's thinking of getting a tattoo! Really? Can you get a tattoo when you're twelve? She reckons she knows somewhere but you'd have to pretend you're older. We were asking her what she'd get. She reckons she wants a seahorse on her ankle. Then we discussed what we'd all have if we got tattoos. Alice said a mermaid on her calf. I said a rose on my wrist and Meg said a heart on her bum! So, we teased her about Will and showing him the heart on her bum. We were all laughing like constipated horses under the duvets. Good job it was dark, otherwise I bet Meg's blushing would have set the place on fire!! Alice said she didn't have any secrets. (Likely story). Then they started asking me about Evil Eve. What could I say? I didn't want to sound like I was keen on her or anything, so I went on about how awful she was. Now I think about it, I sounded just like Mum. I was using all her phrases. Not really what I was thinking at all. I guess my secret is that I actually want to go back there, and tonight I'm thinking of a way I can get Mum and Dad to take notice of me. It's about time they listened to my opinion and what I want. Maybe this Family Mediation thing should include me. I might ask if I can go with them next time.

Anyway, last night was brilliant, but I best get to sleep. School in eleven hours! Great!

Goodnight!

Wednesday 7th March

Today I finally plucked up the courage to talk to Mum and Dad about what I want; going to the Family Mediation thing with them. I've been thinking about it for over a week - what to say and stuff. I've talked it through with Zoe, loads. Surprisingly, she had some good ideas and took it quite seriously. She said I should be really firm and tell them I need my voice to be heard in all this. I shouldn't let them talk me out of it and I have to try not to shout, even if they get shouty, like they do all the time. I should be more mature than them. She reckoned it would show them how they should behave. Definitely.

So, tonight, Dad came to pick Nat and I up from school. He gets Nat first at 3.15 then comes to St. Aidan's. We went for tea to this café in town. It was nice, as usual. Nat always asks him about Eve and he always says she's missing us and wishes we could come back soon. He tells Nat he's working on it, but to be fair, he never bad-mouths Mum in front of us. All the time my stomach was doing cartwheels, because I was building up to having a serious talk with them when he took us home. I was quieter than usual and I couldn't eat much of my meal, but Dad didn't seem to notice.

When we got in the car to come home, I said, 'Dad, can you come in for a few minutes when you drop us off?'

He did a little ironic laugh and said, 'I doubt it, Lou.'

'I want to talk to you and Mum together,' I said.

'Oh, sounds serious,' he replied.

'It is,' I said.

'We can ask Mum. Have you asked her already?'

'No,' I said.

He shrugged. 'I'm not sure she'll let me in and I can't be long. I've got to get back for a conference call with someone for work.'

My face fell and he must have noticed because he added, 'We'll give it a try though.'

When we got to the door I felt sick. I tried to remember what Zoe had said about being firm. Mum opened the door with her usual stony face that she saves specially for Dad. Nat gave her a hug and ran through to the lounge to watch telly. 'Can Dad come in for a minute?' I asked. 'I need to talk to you both.'

Mum raised her eyebrows and opened the door wider. 'I guess so. But only for a minute.'

We went into the kitchen. Dad loitered in the doorway and Mum turned to the washing up. 'So, what's this about?' she said, running the water into the sink.

'Well,' I began. My throat suddenly turned to sandpaper and I had to clear it several times. 'I...' Zoe's voice was in my head, urging me to stick up for myself. 'I want to be included in the discussions about me and Nat. I want to come to Family Mediation.'

Mum turned round and stopped the tap. 'That's not possible. It's only for adults.'

I looked confused. The title suggested it was for the family.

'We could arrange for you to talk to a counsellor, if that would help,' Mum said.

'No, that's not what I want.'

'It might help you to express your feelings, Lou,' Dad added.

'I can ring the counselling service tomorrow and get an appointment,' Mum said.

I said. 'No! What I'm saying is...'

Dad talked over me. 'Yes, that's a good idea. You'd really benefit from it, Lou. I'm glad you talked to us about it. Well done.'

'Yes, it must have taken courage, Lou. Well done,' Mum added.

'Now, I really must shoot off,' Dad said. He kissed the top of my head. 'Bye love.'

Mum came and put her arm round me. .

I wanted to shout at them, but Zoe had told me, 'No getting shouty.' They hadn't listened at all. They'd just

heard what they wanted to hear and thought of an easy solution – she can talk to someone else and everything will be okay. No! However, they had been on the same side for once and that was a good thing. So, I kept quiet. I'll just have to find another way to make them listen.

I messaged Zoe to tell her.

Zoe: 😫
Me: IKR So annoying
Zoe: How u gonna get their attention now?
Me: Dunno. Keep trying. Maybe talk separately
Zoe: Gud luck
Me: 😞 x

Thursday 29th March

I've been trying for weeks to get Mum and Dad to listen to me about what I want. Actually, it's what Nat and I want. I talked to Nat about it, just the two of us, and she said she really wants to go back to Dad's and see Eve. Of course, I knew this. She says it every week to Dad, but I wanted to know if she's just trying to make him happy by saying it. She convinced me that she's not. That made me more determined than ever to make them listen. I've tried talking to Mum on her own, but she's usually doing something else and not really listening. I've tried talking to Dad when we're out, but I don't want him or Nat getting all upset in public, so I usually chicken out.

The divorce is still going ahead. We hear Mum on the phone about it sometimes to solicitors and to Grandma. Nat gets really upset about it. She cries a lot in her room, especially at bed-time. Tonight, she clung to Mum and begged her to persuade Dad to come home. Mum cuddled her and tried to help her get used to the idea that Dad was not coming back. I think it's weird how Nat can really like Eve but wish Dad would come back and live with Mum at the same time. I think I've accepted that he's not coming back, but that doesn't mean I'm okay with it, Dear Diary.

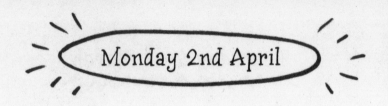

Monday 2nd April

Guess what?
Big shock tonight.

Eve turned up on our doorstep.

I answered the door. Should have seen my face!
'Hi Lou. Is your mum in? I want to talk to her.'
My heart started to pound and my mouth went all dry. I kept the door half shut.
'I don't think she'll talk to you. Can I give her a message?'
Eve was calm and smiley. 'No, not really. I'd like to speak to her face to face.'
Face to face? Yikes! Was this going to be a showdown? Guns ready. Take three paces, turn, shoot! I heard Zoe cackle in my head, with her wicked stepmother voice that I'd not heard for a long time. I felt like Snow White opening the door to the Queen, disguised as the 'innocent' old pedlar lady, who gave her the poisoned apple.
Just as I was trying to find the words to persuade Eve to go away, Mum came up behind. No! Go away, I thought. But it was too late.
'Who is it, Lou?'
At this point, Eve pushed the door open properly.

'Hello Linda. Can we talk?' She was smiling as she said this. I looked at Mum in kind of dumb-struck horror. Mum put on that stony face she usually keeps for Dad!

'Nothing to say to you!' Mum said. 'Now please leave.'

Eve was determined to say what she'd come to say. She wanted Mum to give her another chance and to let us come back to their house for a weekend. She laid it on thick about how Dad was really missing us. That didn't help. It just made Mum all self-righteous about how he shouldn't have left us then. As Mum started to get loud and shouty, Nat came out of the lounge. I could see she wanted to smile and talk to Eve, but she didn't dare.

'Mum!' I said, indicating that Nat was watching her.

'Please just go!' she said and closed the door on Eve.

Nat and I didn't know what to do. Mum stormed into the kitchen without a word, and slammed the door. Tears welled in Nat's eyes, so I put my arm round her. 'Grown-ups are stupid, Nat.' A pretty hopeless thing to say, but I didn't know what else to say. And besides, it was true.

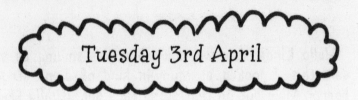

Tuesday 3rd April

Dear Diary,

Today, I have come up with **A PLAN!**
Zoe came back to mine for tea. We went up to my bedroom and chatted about friends, school, clothes, music... the usual. Then we started discussing the situation about me and Nat wanting to go back to Dad's. We were trying to think of a way I could get their attention. Zoe was in her element this morning when I told her what happened last night. She said her mum would have gone mental too and probably punched her dad's floozie (as she calls her). I can't imagine Mum ever doing anything like that!

We were messing around with my hair stuff and make-up. Zoe always looks fab and she's not scared to be different. She doesn't care what anyone else thinks of her either. She has jet black, spiky hair and spends ages every morning gelling it and getting it to look just right. She always wears make up for school too. She's been told to wash it off so many times but she always comes back the next day with it. Even when she got detention, then got sent home, it didn't put her off. In the end the school just gave up trying. She's had both ears pierced twice too, but at least she only wears studs to school.

I was lying on the bed, with my head upside down over the edge and Zoe was back-combing my hair, when she suddenly said, 'You should do something different with your hair.'

I pulled myself up and looked in the mirror. Apart from looking a bit crazy at the moment, it was a bit boring just having long, straight mousy hair. 'Shall I do it like this for school?' I said.

'Nah. Dye it black. And cut it short. You could look this cool too.' She made a stupid face and pointed to her spiky hair. 'We could be twins. Go on Lou. Do something RAD-I-CAL! I dare you.'

I tried to imagine myself with black, punky hair; or maybe a bit of a Goth look. Would it go with blue eyes?

'My mum would cut it for you,' Zoe offered.

I thought dubiously of Zoe's mum's idea of fashionable.

'Erm... don't know. Mum and Dad would go mad.'

'Brilliant! Then you will have achieved your goal. You will have finally got their attention!'

I paused, looking back in the mirror. It could be fun and it would be hilarious to see the expression on Mum and Dad's faces. So, I said, 'Yeah okay. When?'

'I'll ask my mum when she can do it. Maybe next week? You bring the dye, I'll tell my mum. She'll love doing it.'

Later, at the door, as Zoe was leaving, she couldn't resist one of her cackles. 'See ya, Snow White. You might get to see that wicked stepmother again soon. Mwah hah hah!!'

Nat had come to say bye. 'She is mad,' she said. 'Why's she calling you Snow White?'

I shrugged, and told her that it was just from a joke at school today, but I was slightly relieved that she'd gone. What have I signed up for? I'd better not chicken out though. I'd never live it down, because already she's created a group chat and told Alice and Meg what I'm going to do. This is how it went.

Zoe: Hey. Guess what? Lou is gonna cut her hair, dye it black and spike it, like mine. We gonna B like twins!
Alice: CWL!
Meg: Awesome!
Me: IKR
Alice: U gnna look so different
Meg: Can't wait 2 C it
Zoe: We gnna B mazin 2getha
Me: IKR 😊

So, I've got to go through with it now.

Yikes!

Wednesday 4th April

Today, Zoe told me her Mum can do my hair next Thursday after school.

Then she laughed and said, 'You gonna actually do it then?'

I had to say yes to that, didn't I?

She said, 'Never thought you'd go through with it. You still might chicken out.'

'I won't,' I protested, not feeling so sure. 'You'll see. You can come with me to buy the stuff after school.'

She was really excited. 'I'd love to see your mum's face when she sees it. Can I come and watch? Then again, she'd just blame me so maybe not. She can be so boring, your mum. Great temper though.'

I felt a bit defensive of Mum at that point, but all I said was, 'I can't wait to see her face either. She isn't going to stop me doing this. When she finds out, there will be nothing she can do.'

I am sort of looking forward to next Thursday. I've asked Mum if I can go to Zoe's for tea after school. She said fine, but I don't think she even knew what she was agreeing to. She was furiously texting someone. She's still totally pre-occupied with fuming about Dad and Eve. I forgot to tell you about the ear-ache he got down the phone the night Eve came round.

Earlier on this evening I went to see Nat in her room. 'Mum's in a bad mood as usual.' She said.

'Yeah, I know, but she can't stop us doing everything.

I'm sick of her not listening to what we want. She's going to get such a shock next Thursday. She'll have to take notice of me then.'

'Why?'

'Just wait and see. You'll think it's wicked!'

She started pleading with me. 'Tell me. Go on. I'll be your best friend.'

I wished I hadn't told her, all of a sudden. 'Don't be silly, Nat. I can't tell you, in case you let it slip by accident. Just trust me.'

She looked a bit huffily at me. 'Well I'm going to do something too.'

I laughed. 'What?'

'It's a secret. You'll have to wait and see,' she said.

I smiled and gave her a playful shove off her bed. 'Okay. Can't wait!'

I ran out of the room, laughing, before she could get her own back.

Thursday 12th April

The big day has arrived. I've been psyching myself up to it over the last few days and I've got other ideas too...

Tell you about it later tonight, Dear Diary.

Got to get to school.

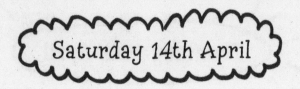

Saturday 14th April

Dear Diary,

A lot has happened since Thursday morning. I couldn't write about it 'til now, but I'm going to write it all down, for you now. Here's the story...

Yesterday, after school, I took Zoe into town.
'Okay, first we need the hair colour.'
We searched the hundreds of boxes of colour all trying to allure me to use them. The titles are hilarious. Honey Gold, Summer Blonde, Hazelnut Whirl, Red Corvette, Ice Shimmer, the list went on. We found the black range. I mean, how can you have a 'black range'? Black is black, isn't it? Anyway, after about twenty minutes of indecisiveness, Zoe forced me to go for Midnight Rendez Vous.
'Right, let's get back to mine,' she said, when we were outside the shop.
'Not yet. Got something else to do first. Come on.'
She started to ask questions, but I just gave her a wicked grin and kept walking. We arrived outside a shop. On the sign it said, Rod's Tattoo and Piercing Parlour.
'You're not!' Zoe exclaimed. I raised my eyebrows at her and grinned.
We went in.
I looked around at the photographs covering the

walls, advertising tattoos that you could have. There were all sorts, from neat little Dolphins and hearts to huge works of art sprawling across muscled chests and arms.

A man, wearing a vest top, his arms covered in tattoos, came over to us, grinning. 'Can I help you ladies?'

I gulped. Zoe flashed him her most flirtatious smile. I swallowed hard, and, trying to sound confident, said, 'Yes, I'd like my ears pierced twice, please, and a silver stud in my nose.'

He raised his eyebrows and looked me up and down, in my neat school uniform. Then he turned to Zoe, in her not so neat uniform, plastered in make-up and nodded knowingly. 'Your idea, is it?'

'No way!' She said, holding her hands up as if in surrender. 'Hey, if she wants to do it I'm with her all the way, but it's definitely NOT my idea.'

He looked at me again. 'You sure you want all that at once? It'll be really sore.' He gestured towards my uniform. 'What's the school going to say? Bet you'll get into trouble.'

'Not just with school,' Zoe laughed.

'How old are you? Do your parents know?' he asked.

I started to worry that he was going to refuse, so I pulled myself up tall and pretended I was Zoe. 'Look, do you want the business or not? I'll go get it done somewhere else if you don't,' I said, surprising myself.

'Okay then,' the man said. 'At least I know you'll get a professional job done if I do it myself. Come and sit down. I've got some Hello mags over there your friend can read.'

'Cool,' Zoe said, leaping into the squashy leather sofa in the corner.

When we stood outside the shop not long afterwards, two silver studs throbbed in each ear lobe. My nose felt like it had been stung by a killer bee! Zoe was trying hard not to laugh and to be sympathetic to my pain. I think she was genuinely impressed.

'You'll look really good, Lou, when the redness goes down. The silver nose stud is gorgeous.'

'Thanks,' I said, putting on a brave face. 'Let's get to your house.'

'Are you sure you still want to do that as well?'

'Why does everybody keep asking me if I'm sure? Yes! I'm sure. Come on let's get on with it.'

Zoe's mum, Lisa, smiled when she saw me. 'Well, well. You certainly are going for a change of image, Lou. It looks great. What are we doing with the hair then?'

'I want to go really short. Layered and a bit spiky on top (maybe not as much as Zoe's), but over my ears. Short wispy fringe. Here, like this.'

I produced a picture of a model I'd cut out of a magazine. I hadn't even shown it to Zoe. 'Do you think you can do it?'

'Of course I can,' Lisa said. 'I am a hairdresser, Lou. You've got to trust me.'

'I do, I do. And I'll pay you for it, when I get some

more cash. Just spent most of mine.'

'Nah, it's on the house. You're my Zoe's best friend. Take it as a present, to help you through your mum and dad's divorce and all that stuff.'

'Thanks,' I said. 'Do you think it'll suit me?'

She studied the picture for some moments, then she studied me. 'Yeah, I think it will. You might not think so at first though, it'll be dramatic. But our Zoe will help you with some make-up to suit the style and you'll look fab.'

I took a deep breath. 'Do it.'

*

My mum was going to FREAK! If she even recognised me that is! As I walked home from Zoe's, I kept touching my bare neck. It felt cold, after having long hair. I also kept catching glimpses of myself in shop windows and having to reassure myself that it actually was me! My piercings had stopped throbbing and didn't appear so angry. I thought I looked quite cool. Zoe's mum had done a great job on my hair and Zoe had made me up and given me a look verging on Gothic: Very red lips, heavy black eyeliner and dark eyeshadow. It suited me. Pity I was still in my school uniform. As I reached the door of my house, I hesitated. There was no going back. I ran my tongue over my teeth, tossed my head back and entered.

'Hi Mum,' I shouted casually.

No answer, but I could hear her on the phone. As I entered the kitchen she had her back to me. She was just ending the call. She turned: The moment of truth...

She looked panicked. Was it really that bad? 'Lou, it's Natalie. She's...' Then her mouth fell open. She stopped and stared.

'What the... What have you done!'

I'd have thought that was obvious, but I was more concerned with what she had been about to say. 'What do you mean,' it's Nataile?" I said.

Mum shook her head. 'She's gone missing. I went up to her room about half an hour ago, and she was gone! I've looked everywhere for her. I've searched the garden, I've looked in the street, I've tried the neighbours. Your Dad's on his way over.'

Mum was distraught. Tears spilled down her cheeks. I felt a fool. All the impact of my transformation faded into insignificance.

I remembered what Nat had said last week. 'She planned this,' I mumbled, almost to myself.

'What? How do you know?'

'She told me she was planning something but that it was a secret.'

Mum was furious now. 'Well, why didn't you get it out of her?'

I felt stupid. I mumbled, 'Cos I wouldn't tell her what I was planning.'

At that moment, Mum burst like a water-balloon. 'How childish, Louise! I can't believe you've done this.' She wafted her hand up and down to indicate my appearance. 'I'll deal with *this* later. She's taken Poops, her backpack and coat. I can't see anything else missing. Now think! Where would she go?'

'Have you tried her school friends?'

'I was just about to.'

'I'll get my bike and go look round the streets and the park. Try not to panic, I'm sure she won't have gone far.'

Mum ignored me. She was already calling all the parents she knew. I went to get my bike, rubbing the stupid red lipstick off my mouth as I went and messaging Zoe.

Me: Nat's gone missing!

Zoe didn't reply straight away, which was annoying. Where was she, just when I needed her most?

I knew some of Nat's favourite places. I couldn't believe she had planned to run away. I never thought she'd be brave (or stupid) enough to do something like this. But then, who am I to talk? Look at me. I rode round the park, the school... I even went down the woods where we're not supposed to go on our own. I must admit I was a bit scared of going in there by myself. It was starting to get dark by this time and I didn't want to go into the woods by myself. I shouted her name a few times. I didn't think she'd be in there. She wasn't that brave. Where could she have gone? She must be at a friend's house. I looked at my phone. Still no word from Zoe. I headed home.

When I got back Dad had arrived. Mum was truly

in panic mode. And she was talking to Dad as if he'd never been gone these past few months. 'Oh Mike, what are we going to do? I should call the police. I can't understand it. Not Nat.'

He said, 'We've got to concentrate on finding her, then we can sort out why she's done it.' It was a big mistake to say that.

'I think it's obvious, isn't it?' Mum said, giving him a hard look.

But Dad stayed calm. 'Let's not start throwing blame around now. It's not helpful.'

At this point, he turned to see me standing at the kitchen door. He gawped at me and tried to suppress a smile. 'Wow! That's some change of image.'

'Is that all you can say?' Mum said. 'She is in big trouble later, when we've found Nat.'

'Yes, of course,' Dad said, not wanting to contradict Mum at this point.

Mum hadn't had any success with Nat's friends, although one of the mums said that Nat had told her daughter that she was going to 'teach Mum and Dad a lesson.' I told them all the places I'd been to and that there was no sign of her. I'd asked a few people on the street if they'd seen her, but no one had.

Mum was frantic when I mentioned the woods.

'I'm going to call the police,' Dad said.

By this time, several of our neighbours had come to see if they could help. They were sent out to keep searching the area. The police came within fifteen minutes and were asking Mum and Dad lots of questions.

Mum started crying. Dad kept rubbing his eyebrows, as he tried to stay calm and think. Nat had been missing for at least three hours now and it was completely dark outside. The police were mobilizing search parties. Dad texted Eve to tell her he was not coming home, as he would be staying to help with the search.

I saw this text: *'No sweetheart, I think it's best you don't come here. I'll call as soon as there's any news.'*

Mum was being comforted by a police officer, who was telling her reassuring stories of runaways turning up.

'What can I do, Dad?' I asked. Then I burst into tears. 'This is all my fault.'

He put his arms around me. 'Don't be silly, Lou. How can it be?'

I told him about the conversation last week and me wanting to do something to make them listen and Nat saying she was going to do something too.

Dad pulled a 'don't quite know what to say' face and kissed me on top of my head. 'You can come and search with me. Go and get something warm on and wipe that stuff off your face. You've got black smudges all over your cheeks.' I ran upstairs. 'Bring that big torch, that your mum keeps in her bedside cabinet,' he shouted.

Minutes later we were out on the streets. Mum was left with one police officer, as the others joined Dad and I in the search. We were knocking on doors and asking if we could search people's gardens, garages and outhouses. By midnight there were still no sightings of her. We went home with some of the police officers and Mum made hot drinks. Actually, the officer made the drinks, as Mum was shaking too much. She was sitting at the kitchen table.

I went to hug her. 'You okay, Mum?' I couldn't think of what else to say.

'Of course I'm not,' she snapped, pushing me away.

Dad put a hand gently on Mum's arm. 'Hey, come on, Linda, don't take it out on Lou.'

'Oh, shut up Mike! She put the idea into Nat's head. Get out there and find her. I wish I could, but they say I need to be here for when she comes home.'

I started to cry again. I knew she was right, but it hurt like crazy for her to say it out loud. Dad got angry with Mum then. 'You're being harsh. This is our fault. Don't blame Lou.' Mum didn't reply. She was too lost in her own grief. She just sat there sniffling into a cup of coffee.

Dad and I retreated to the living room. 'What do we do now?' I asked.

Just then the officer drinking tea in the armchair, got a call to his radio. Someone had seen a girl of Nat's description, getting into a car with a woman, at about ten thirty. It appeared suspicious because the girl was so young and seemed hesitant.

Mum was hysterical. 'She's been abducted! Please, no! You've got to find her! Please! Oh God, please bring her back!' With that cry for help to the Almighty, she broke down and flopped onto the sofa, sobbing uncontrollably. I was crying too, and Dad. But, he and the officer moved to comfort Mum. I ran into the kitchen where I paced around, praying silently that we'd get Nat back safely. I'd never forgive myself for this.

I got my phone out. Zoe had replied earlier, but I'd been too busy to look.

> Zoe: Zounds! Have you found her yet?

Her stupid word annoyed me, at a time like this, but at least she cared. There were a lot more messages when I hadn't replied.

> Any news?
> What's happening?
> What's going on?
> Has she turned up yet?
> LMK
> ASAP
> PCM 😵

The messages had stopped around eleven thirty, so I guessed she'd gone to sleep. I replied though, just in case.

> Been a sighting of girl getting into car. Police investigating. Scared 🙁

The police officers didn't have a registration number to check, only the colour and possible make of the car: Red; could have been a Clio or a Peugeot 206.

Dad came into the kitchen with a couple of officers.

They sat down at the table. 'Make us some coffees, love,' Dad said to me. They started to ask Dad a lot of questions about Nat and what was going on in our lives, at the moment. I caught a glimpse of my distorted reflection in the stainless-steel kettle. I got a fright. I'd forgotten how I looked. My nose and ears were throbbing again. I ached to know what was happening to Nat.

Please God, keep her safe...

I wandered into the lounge to check on Mum. It was about two in the morning now. She was lying on the sofa with a blanket over her, clutching a handful of tissues and muttering to herself. The officer, Melanie, was sitting on the arm of the sofa looking helpless, rubbing her arm across Mum's back. She smiled at me.

'Your mum's just resting,' she said in a stage whisper. 'We gave her a little something to calm her down. Could you get some sleep do you think?'

They'd drugged my mum! But maybe that was a good thing. I stared at her, shaking my head. 'Hardly!' I blurted out.

'Sorry, stupid suggestion,' she said.

I felt rude then. 'Would you like a coffee or something?' She said yes.

'What about Mum?' Mum was in some sort of trance, which I later realised was a combination of medication and shock. Melanie shook her head.

Back in the kitchen there had been some more news. A sighting of a similar child in a petrol station on the outskirts of town, buying bread and milk at midnight.

The cashier told police she got back into a red Clio, with a woman driving. They were going through the CCTV footage now. Dad thought it best not to tell Mum. He looked in on her and came back rubbing his eyebrow furiously. His phone rang.

'Hi.' Pause. 'No. But...' He headed upstairs and I didn't hear the rest. I gave Melanie her coffee, slumped down in an armchair, and closed my eyes. Images of Nat crying in the back of a car whirled around my head. What was happening to her? In my mind a big bad wolf was driving the car, dressed as Grandmama. Then an old witch was sitting in the back with Nat, trying to get her to eat an apple. Nat was shaking her head. Then the witch turned into Snow White's wicked stepmother, who was trying to stick a big needle through Nat's nose.

At that moment, Dad gently shook me and handed me a cup of tea. I must have dozed off. A pale light was seeping through the window.

'Have they found her, Dad?' I looked across at Mum. She was asleep. Melanie had disappeared.

'No, but they traced that car. Got the registration from the CCTV. They've located the address it's registered to. It's about seventy miles away. They're on their way there now.'

My heart pounded. I felt like I was going to be sick. I tried to sip my tea and burnt my lip. 'Should we wake Mum?'

Dad looked across at her, and ran his hand across his face. 'Not yet.'

I looked at my phone. Zoe had messaged me.

Zoe: This is really bad. Any news? What's happening now?

Me: Police found the address of the person with the car. Going there now

Zoe: Blundering Blueberries! Scarey! ☹

Me: Yep

Zoe: Don't think I should go to school today. Should I come round?

Me: No. Too many people here. Just keep in touch

Zoe: K LMK news ASAP x

Me: K x

No one spoke. Dad was pacing, texting and muttering, 'Why doesn't she answer?' I guessed he was talking about Eve. He tried to phone her several times but she didn't answer. He left one message. 'Call me.' Stupidly, Zoe's voice came into my mind, cackling her wicked stepmother laugh. I wondered if Eve had a red Clio that Dad knew nothing about.

*

Nothing happened for what seemed forever, then suddenly, the front door burst open. 'I've found her! I've found her!' It was Eve.

Dad and I jumped up. My tea went all over the carpet.

Seeing Eve here, in the house, was almost more startling than what she was saying.

'You've found her? Where? Where is she?' Dad demanded.

The commotion woke Mum. She lurched off the sofa and fell onto the floor.

'What is *she* doing here?' She croaked, trying to pick herself up. I went to help her.

'She's found Natalie, Mum.'

Eve said, 'She's safe. Come and see. She's in my car, asleep.'

By this time the police officers, including Melanie, had come through from the kitchen.

'Get out of my house!' Mum shrieked at Eve. 'We're in the middle of a crisis and I don't want you here.' She launched at Eve.

'Linda!' Dad grabbed Mum by the arms and shouted in her face. The shock hit her like a fist and she fell back onto the sofa. Dad bent down and spoke gently, as if to a toddler. 'Eve has found Nat. She's in the car.' Mum collapsed against Dad in violent sobs.

Everyone crowded round Eve's car. There was Nat, asleep under a blanket. We peered in, like people observing a dangerous animal in the zoo. Then Mum was crying Nat's name and so was I. Dad opened the car and lifted Nat out. She began to stir. Looking up, she saw Dad, smiled and put her arms round his neck. Mum and I hugged them both. Then Dad carried her inside.

There was lots of hugging, kissing and crying all

round. The police radioed that she had been found and later a message came in that the Clio had been a red herring: Just a single mum, on a long journey, out too late at night with a tired and surly child.

As Dad, Mum and I huddled round Nat, I noticed the police lead Eve out of the room. 'What has Lou done to her hair and face?' Nat said.

'Never mind that,' Mum said, half smiling, half scowling. 'Why did you run away, Nat? Where have you been?'

'Lou said she was going to give you two a shock, to make you listen to us, so I wanted to help.'

Mum and Dad gave me a serious stare, the kind you get when you know you're going to be grounded for weeks, have your phone confiscated and lose six months' pocket money.

'But where have you been? We've been worried sick. We thought...' Dad trailed off.

'I walked and walked for ages. Then I sat in a bus shelter and ate my chocolate and had a drink. I was going to come home then, but I realised I'd walked a long way and I didn't know where I was. I was too scared to ask anyone, because you shouldn't talk to strangers. So I kept walking. But then, when it got dark, I decided to find somewhere to sleep, and there was this shop with those big bins out the back, and it looked sheltered, so I curled up between them. Then, I woke up because I was cold, so I started walking again. I was trying to come home, but I couldn't find the way. And then a car pulled up beside me and it was Eve, so I got in.'

'Eve picked you up?' Mum said. She turned to Dad. 'She picked Nat up! She has a red car, like the one at the petrol station. She tried to kidnap our daughter!'

'Don't be ridiculous,' Dad said. 'It's not a Clio and anyway, she found her and brought her back here. Last time I spoke to her she was out in her car, searching. Said she couldn't just sit there doing nothing.'

Mum wasn't listening. She stood up. 'Where is she? Is she still here?'

She headed for the door, despite protests from Dad and Nat. We followed. She found Eve in the kitchen, being questioned by the police. 'She tried to kidnap my daughter. I'll kill her.'

'Linda!' Dad grabbed Mum, who was insane with rage. She thrashed in his grip, but a police officer got up to intervene.

'Get her out of my house!' she screeched, as Melanie and another officer led her back to the lounge.

Dad put his arm round Eve's shoulder. 'It's okay, love. She's in shock. I think it's best if you go home for now. I'll be there soon. You get some sleep. You've done a fantastic thing today.' He hugged her, then looked at the remaining officer. 'It is all right for her to go, isn't it?'

'Yes. It's fine. We'll be in touch.' Eve smiled weakly at us. Nat suddenly clutched her round the waist and Eve stroked her hair briefly.

Dad took Eve to her car. I watched him kiss her and she was gone. The police officers spoke to him, saying they would call tomorrow, then they left. When the four of us were alone and Mum was silently holding Nat, Dad said, ' We need to talk about this, but not now. Let's get some sleep. I'll come round later.' He turned to me. 'Will you be okay?'

'Yes Dad,' I said, responsibly. He helped get me, Nat and Mum into bed, then went home.

Before I went to sleep, I messaged Zoe to say Nat had been found. She was relieved. I slept for ages. And now, it's evening and I'm writing to you, Diary. I feel a lot calmer, but totally drained. Zoe wanted to come round, but I just wanted to be on my own. Nat seems fine. She came in and snuggled up to me earlier. She said she was sorry, but I told her it was my fault and that she didn't need to be sorry, just promise that she'd never do anything like that again. She said she liked my nose stud and earrings and asked if she could get her ears pierced! Oh great.

Zoe messaged me this morning. I'd been telling her how stupid I felt about the hair and piercings etc. She said:

Remember why u did all this in the first place. U wanted their attention. Now U have it so make it count!

We had a family meeting this afternoon.

'It's not our fault!' I protested. (I had decided Zoe was right. I wasn't going to take all the blame.) 'It's you two who should be sorry. You are screwing up our lives. You've left us, Dad, and Mum is trying to stop us seeing you. Mum is always in a bad mood and never listens and you care more about Eve than us!'

Mum and Dad stared at the floor. For once, Mum didn't start ranting at Dad.

'But Nat, honey, that was such a dangerous thing to do,' said Dad.

'We were frantic,' said Mum. 'Don't you know how much we love you?'

There was silence. Then Nat said, 'Mum, I want to go to Dad's house.'

'What, now? You can't live with him. Absolutely not! Not with that...'

'No!' Nat shouted, making us all jump. 'I mean I want to stay with Dad at weekends. I don't want to stop seeing him. And Eve.'

I cringed slightly. Mum winced. Dad raised his eyebrows. More silence. Everyone looked at Mum.

'Me too, Mum,' I said, backing Natalie up.

She paused. 'I'll think about it.'

Dad started up. 'Linda! You really can't stop them coming you know. I can get a court order and....'

'Be quiet!' Nat screeched, putting her hands over her ears.

Mum put her arm around Nat. 'We'll work something out. Now, say goodbye to Dad. He's just leaving. Oh, and Lou - you are grounded.'

'I agree with that,' Dad said.

'At least you agree on something!' I mumbled.

Dad left and I came to talk to you, my Dear Diary.

I just hope that Mum and Dad will start behaving better. It's like a competition to see who can get their own way the most. Nat and I are not possessions. What about what we want? Nat was cool in that meeting. She was braver than me. She's getting pretty stroppy these days. Good for her.

Wonder how long I'm grounded for?

Saturday 21st April

~~~~~~~~~~~~~~~~

Mum and Dad have grounded me for a month. They agreed on that at least! After everything that's happened, I'm not too annoyed about it. Zoe's not even allowed to contact me out of school, as Mum suspects she had an influence on me. Mum insists on checking my phone every night. I guess I could just delete messages (that's what Zoe says I should do), but I'm sticking with Mum and Dad's rules for now, trying to keep in their good books.

Mum wanted me to take the studs out, but I convinced her they would get infected and I'd end up a mess. She wrote to the school apologizing and absolving herself of blame. She made me write too. Just as well though, because I reckon it got me out of a week's detentions.

My friends really liked what I'd done. I got some snide remarks from some of the 'populars', who think everyone else is scum compared to them. But I just held my nerve, like Zoe would do, and thought of something witty to say back. Zoe joined in and we ended up having some brilliant laughs at their expense.

*

Mum took some persuading this week, and plenty of grovelling from Dad, to give Eve yet another chance, but she has given in. Nat is becoming very persistent these days. So, today we came to Dad's. It's the Easter holidays and Mum has said we can stay over for a few days.

Wow!

She gave us our Easter Eggs this morning to take with us. She'd bought us our favourites.

*

Eve seemed really pleased to see us and said she loved my new image. I didn't have so much make-up on and she said it suited me. She was a bit careful around Dad, as she knew he'd agreed to ground me for it. But when he was out of the room, she told me what she really thought.

'I love what you've done with your hair, Lou. It looks great. Really sophisticated. And the piercings are great. Love the silver nose stud. I've got a couple you can have if you like them, for when you can take that one out. Better not get anything else pierced for a while though, eh?' We shared a conspiratorial (oooh, good word) smile.

Eve and Dad asked us if we'd like to decorate the spare room; to personalise it. They've put bunk beds in there and we got really excited about making it ours. We did some designs together with Eve. She's so talented. She said loads of nice things to Nat about her drawings, which made Nat dead happy because she loves drawing and colouring. Eve said my designs were brilliant and she could really see us bringing it all to life.

We went out and bought paint, then made a start on changing the colour of the walls. Eve thought it was a great idea when I suggested an under-sea mural.

So, guess what colour the walls are now? Yes, pink of course, Dear Diary! No, don't be daft. We found this lovely aquamarine colour. Eve said it matched my eyes. Not sure about that.

I was nervous that something bad might happen, but it didn't and we were all relieved. Nat seemed completely chilled with Eve. So, that made me relax too. Could be a fun weekend. Soooo tempted to message Zoe, cos Dad won't check. But I decided to be good. Very difficult.

Polish my halo!

Happy Easter, Dear Diary,

We got more yummy Easter Eggs! Biggest ones I've ever had. I think Eve bought them. She told Nat to go easy on them! No more puking please! LOL

We spent most of the day painting. When we finished, Dad looked like he'd been painting himself more than the walls. He told me that Eve was an artist. She drew that picture of the daisy chain girl that's hanging over their fireplace. I'd never thought to ask what Eve did. I'd never thought about the fact that she was a real person, with a life apart from just being my dad's girlfriend. I asked her to show me some of her artwork. It was amazing! There was lots of stuff from her student days, as well as designs she'd submitted for publication. There were watercolours, pastels, pencil drawings, charcoal, batik. She certainly is talented. She said she was a freelance artist and had done designs for all sorts of things, from greetings cards to CD covers, even patterned kitchen towels! She said she'd love to help us with the room if we wanted her to. I thought that would be cool. We had a good laugh together today. We played board games this evening too. Wanted to tell Zoe about it, but still being good. Can't believe I'm not even going to see her for the next couple of weeks.

Tuesday 24th April

We came home this morning. We've had such a good time and can't wait to go back and work on the mural. Nat was so excited that she told Mum all about it. Mum sulked about it for ages, as Nat and I chattered on and on about what we wanted to do. She didn't ask any questions and just made grunting noises.

I enjoy art at school and I'm going to collect pictures of sea creatures while we're on school holidays, to practice drawing them. Nat wants to do it too, so I suppose it will be good for us to do it together since I'm not allowed to see my friends. That is going to be tough, now there's no school for two weeks. I'm going to be so bored.

Really want to talk to Zoe. Still being good. How???

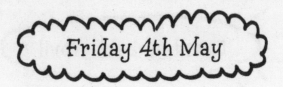

Friday 4th May

Hello Diary,

This school hols have been *sooooo* boring! Apart from Nat's birthday on Monday, nothing much has happened. Mum made her a really lovely cake in the shape of a Barbie castle and let her have four friends round all day. They were completely wild and screechy, so I hid in my room with my earphones in.

And I have a confession. I gave in and have been messaging Zoe, Alice and Meg for a few days. To be honest, Mum has stopped checking. She's forgotten about it. I did ask if I could go out at one point, but she still refused, even when I went on and on about being bored. To be fair, she did take us to the cinema and the beach over the last week too. But I'm desperate to see my friends. It's been getting me down seeing what they're all up to, on Instagram, and feeling left out.

Dad came over for Nat's birthday and took us to Pizza Hut, where we met Eve. We talked about the mural a lot.

Nat and I persuaded Mum to let us go to Dad's this weekend. I think she was glad of the space after having us around 24/7 for the last two weeks. So, Dad is picking us up soon and we can get on with our painting. We've got a collage of pictures off the internet; like dolphins, clown fish, seahorses (my favourite), anemones (hard to spell, had to look it up), and we've done lots of sketches too. Can't wait to show Eve.

May Bank Holiday Weekend

Dear Diary,

We spent most of the weekend decorating the room. We had a brilliant time. Dad was tea-boy and general dogsbody, while us girls got on with the creative stuff. When it was finished, it looked ace. Dad was well impressed. The sea-bed was painted with anemones, sea urchins, crabs and starfish. There were dolphins swimming near the top of the room and a couple of Clown Fish with a Blue Tang tagging along. (Are you impressed I know what kind of fish Dory is? Okay, I looked it up). We also painted a shoal of bright yellow fish and Eve painted a ship-wreck with a menacing looking shark peeking out of it. It was sooooo cool!

I was taking pictures on my phone to share with my friends. All of them commented and loads of other people saw them too.

Meg: Awesome!
Alice: Amazing!
Zoe: I want one!

'Can we take a picture to show Mum?' Nat begged. Dad and Eve looked a bit

unsure. 'Please, please!'

Dad took some pictures on his phone too. He didn't want to send them to Mum from his phone, so he printed them off so Nat could stick them up in her room at home.

*

Nat was full of it when we got back this afternoon. She thrust the photos into Mum's hand.

'Look at our new room, isn't it brilliant Mum? I painted that crab there and Eve helped me paint that dolphin. I painted the sea too and did some of those starfish stencils.'

Mum listened and held the pictures while Nat talked. She never smiled once. 'Yes, it's very nice,' and 'Well done love.' was all she said. I talked about it a little, but thought that I should play it down. Inside I was as bubbly as Nat about it. We'd had a brilliant time doing it and Eve had been great fun. She was also a very good teacher. She'd shown us lots of things about drawing and painting we'd never learn at school. But Mum was distant. I know it's hard for her. Will try to keep off the subject of Dad and Eve as much as possible.

Later, I told Nat not to talk about Eve, Dad or our new room in front of Mum anymore.

'It's not like Eve's our Mum, is it?' she said. 'She's just Dad's girlfriend. Like a big sister really. And our room is great.' I gave her a look, so she said, 'But I won't talk about it in front of Mum.'

Tuesday 8th May

First day back at school today. I was desperate to see my friends again. I was getting used to my short hair now, but was a bit nervous in case anyone decided to have a go at me again. It was fine in the end. The ones who were horrible before Easter had moved on to other things and found other people to say stupid things to. It was *sooooo* good to be back with Alice, Meg and Zoe, even if I did have to put up with boring school to see them.

Dear Diary,

Just thought you should know that Nat and I are being the best daughters ever! All week we've both tried to be super nice to Mum. I've kept my room tidy and offered to do some washing up twice. I even brought her a cup of tea and snuggled up to her on the sofa tonight, after Nat was in bed.

'So, what's all this in aid of?' she asked.

'What?' I replied, faking innocence.

'Being extra nice to me,' she smiled. 'I can't remember the last time I was honoured with a cuddle from my eldest daughter.'

'Don't you like it?' I said.

She said, 'Of course I do. I just wondered what I'd done to deserve it.'

I know it's a bit cringey, but I said, 'Well... you're just a great Mum, isn't that enough?'

She put her arm around me and squeezed me. Then she smiled the best smile I've seen her do for ages. We watched TV together for the rest of the night and had a laugh.

Saturday 12th May

Big news today, Dear Diary. When we saw Dad and Eve, they sat us down on the sofa, opposite the daisy chain girl, while they stood nervously together. We looked expectantly at them. It was very like when we first met Eve. They were making me nervous.

'Your Dad and I have something to tell you.'

My stomach lurched.

'It's good news, don't worry!' Eve looked at Dad. 'Go on Mike,' she smiled, nudging him with her elbow.

'We've got engaged!' he blurted out, thrusting Eve's left hand high in the air. On her finger was a beautiful engagement ring. He grinned manically at us.

We both stared open-mouthed. Whoa! Engaged! But Mum and Dad weren't even divorced yet. This seemed too fast. Nat looked from Dad to Eve to me, totally bewildered. I asked the questions and made the objections.

'But, how can you be engaged? You're still married to Mum.'

'Well, the divorce is nearly through now. We got the decree nisi this week, which is a posh way of telling us that it's almost finalised,' explained Dad.

Finalised? This was it. Dad and Mum, finished. Mum home alone, Dad here with Eve. No going back. Forever. Eve would be our new stepmother. Zoe was just about to cackle in my head (a sound that had long faded from my mind), when I stopped her with another question.

'But isn't it illegal or something, before you're actually divorced? I mean, what if you and Mum decide to get back together?' I couldn't believe I was saying this. I'd known for ages that they weren't going to get back together. Dad was obviously head over heels with Eve. So why was I saying such stupid things?

'Lou, soon Mum and I are not going to be married anymore. That's a fact. But we're still going to be your Mum and Dad. Nothing is ever going to change that. Nothing! We'll still love you just the same and...'

Suddenly, Eve bent forward and took Nat's hands in hers. Big tears were rolling down Nat's face.

'Aw, little Nat. I'm sorry,' she gulped. Then Eve was in tears too. Then I burst into tears, then Dad. We ended up squashed together into a big, wet ball of hug.

Eve found a box of tissues and Dad took Nat on his knee. 'Darling, things will be good again, you'll see. They're getting easier all the time, aren't they? You have three grown-ups now, who love you very much.'

Nat was still sniffling. 'But Daddy, I want you and Mummy to be married. I don't want you to marry Eve.' Then turning to Eve, she added, 'I do like you Eve, but I want Mummy and Daddy to be married.' Dad didn't know what to say. He just cuddled her tightly into him.

I'm dreading telling Mum. In fact, should I tell her? Maybe Dad doesn't want her to know until the divorce is final. He should tell her, really. He probably doesn't want me to tell her. I had to tell someone though.

Me: Dad has got engaged to Eve!

Zoe: Zoopendidliocious!

Me: 😵

Zoe: Soz. When?

Me: Told us 2day. Got ring on

Zoe: What's it like?

Me: Sparkly! Nat upset

Zoe: She'll get over it

Me: Heartless!

Zoe: That's me!

Zoe: What d'u think?

Me: Dunno. OK bout it I guess

Zoe: U seem 2 get on with her

Me: Yeah

Zoe: Watch out 4 the wicked bit though. All of em are nice on the surface! Mwah hah hah!

Me: Shut up!

Zoe: ROFL

Me: Anyway, all the wicked stepmothers I've read about are horrible from the beginning.

Zoe: Only because the dad is dead – Snow White, Cinderella. Babes in the wood one pretends 2 B nice – picnic in woods – oh dear they got lost, wicked witch blah blah blah

Me: What U like? Eve is fine

Zoe: Hope so, for your sake

Me: So melodramatic! ROFL

Zoe: 😁

I asked Dad if he is going to tell Mum.

'Course I'm going to tell her, love. I wouldn't expect you to take that on. Goodness knows how she'll react.

But maybe she'll be fine. She doesn't want me back. And she's been so good about letting you two come over since' (he made air quotes with his fingers) "the incidents."

'Maybe I should help you Dad,' I suggested. 'She might be better if she sees I'm okay about it.'

Dad looked at me for a moment with his face all screwed up. 'And are you okay about it? I mean really okay?'

'I think I am,' I replied. 'Anyway, I'll fit in better at school now that I'm from a split family, with a wicked stepmother!'

I laughed but he only smiled, sadly.

Sunday 13th May

Dear Diary, thought I'd tell you how Mum took the news.

When he took us home this evening, Dad said he had something to tell Mum. I installed Nat in front of her favourite DVD, then went to the kitchen. They had waited for me and I joined them round the table feeling far too grown up. Dad broke the news, as gently as he could, then took a deep breath and drew back, as if waiting for the barrage of abuse. Mum was silent, staring into her coffee. Dad and I just watched and waited for her to do something.

After what seemed a very long time, she looked up and sighed. Her eyes were watery but she didn't cry. 'I was expecting it, if I'm honest. Only I thought you'd wait until we were divorced. Why do you have to get engaged so soon? Is there more news you're waiting to tell me?' She raised her eyebrows at Dad.

'No, no, nothing like that. We just… we want to get married and I wanted to… make it official.' He pushed his hands through his hair and sighed. 'Oh, it feels wrong saying this to you.'

Mum shrugged. 'Yes, well. What's right and wrong got to do with anything? I don't really know anymore.'

Dad stood up. I hadn't said anything the whole time and it was as if they had forgotten I was there. So, I quickly thought of something. 'Nat and I will be okay. I mean, we'll get used to the idea.' They both looked at me, remembering I was there at last.

'Thanks Lou.' Dad smiled, kissing me on the cheek. Mum squeezed my hand.

When Dad left, Mum went upstairs. She stayed there for a long time. Her eyes and nose were very red when she came downstairs. Nat and I gave her a big hug. Then Nat said something which made her smile.

'You know Mummy,' she began very seriously, 'We'll always love you, even when you and Dad are not married anymore. You'll always be our Mummy. Eve's okay, but we love you the best.'

Mum smiled and cried and laughed all at the same time.

Friday 1st June

My Dear Diary,

I'm so sorry I haven't written to you for a while. I've been wrapped up in school work and revision for the millions of tests we've been having. (Boring). On the weekends, I've mainly been at Dad and Eve's, with a couple of Saturdays in town with Alice, Meg and Zoe. That was good because Dad picked me up and we went back to his, so I still got to see him.

Big news that I missed telling you is... the divorce came through just after Dad had announced his engagement. Mum joked about being a free woman and being able to do anything she liked now, but since then she's been spending a lot of time by herself. She didn't go out at all except to work. Her friends phone, but I often hear her turning down invitations to meet up with them. Some weekends she doesn't get out of bed until midday. She's becoming a bit of a recluse. I don't know what to do. I wonder if I should tell Dad. But what can he do about it? And Mum wouldn't listen to him. She'd just start telling him it was all his fault anyway. Dad and Eve are wrapped up in planning their future. What's left for Mum? And Nat and I get to bounce between the two of them, trying to be what each of them want us to be. I'm happy for Dad but sad for Mum, and I can't help blaming him for making her feel this way.

The divorce itself hasn't made much impression on

Nat, as, in many ways, it hasn't really changed day to day arrangements. We are still mainly going to Dad's on Saturdays, staying overnight and coming home Sunday. Sometimes Dad comes over and takes us out for tea mid-week. Sometimes we're one of those families sitting in MacDonald's, with only their Dad. I realise now that they aren't as unhappy as I'd first thought, that day when everything fell apart.

I'm going to keep an eye on Mum and if she doesn't start picking up I'll have to find someone to talk to about it. Maybe I'll have to ring Grandma, but she lives a long way away, so I don't know if she could help anyway. She might have some ideas though.

Thursday 14th June

Happy birthday to me,
Happy birthday to me,
Happy birthday dear meeeeeeeeeeee,
Happy birthday to me!

Yay!
The big

13

I am now officially a teenager. All my friends are already thirteen. I'm the baby of the bunch. I got some great presents at school today. Zoe bought me some really nice earrings and nose studs. I tried them tonight. The nose ones have different coloured glass, like diamonds, in them. They're so cute. Alice bought me these gorgeous smellies and Meg got me this eye shadow palette with all the colours I love. A few other people gave me presents and cards too. My form tutor even got me a card and some chocolate. Mum made me a cake that looked like a phone. She's so good at cakes. I took pics of it to post on Instagram. And my main present from Mum and Dad (they clubbed together) was a new phone. (Appropriate cake, see?)

I've spent most of the evening playing around getting to know it. Love it. We did go out for a meal too. Mum and Dad came together. No Eve, of course, but she had signed the card from her and Dad and put a nice message in it. It was a bit awkward at first, with Mum and Dad having to make polite conversation. This is the first time Mum has been out in ages. We did manage to have a laugh, though. Even Mum laughed at some of Dad's terrible jokes. I'm having a party at the weekend with loads of friends. We've hired the Rec Hall. It's going to be great. Can't wait.

Saturday 16th June

Dear Diary,

It's nearly midnight and I'm sooooo tired! But I've had an amazing night! My party was wicked! Mum and Dad had to be there, but they kept out of the way most of the time. I had warned Dad not to come in and embarrass me by doing any 'Dad Dancing.' He did threaten to, at one point, but Mum rescued me by grabbing him into the kitchen and keeping him out of the way.

We all danced and danced and danced. Well, the girls did, anyway. The boys mainly ran around bursting balloons, eating most of the food and being stupid. Meg dared me to go up to Will Duggan and tell him Zoe likes him. So I did, and he nearly ran a mile. Zoe never found out or she'd kill me. I did see Will and some of the others pointing at Zoe later, and they weren't laughing or anything, so maybe he likes her too. I really like this boy called Josh Cole. He's one of Will's friends. But thankfully I've not told any of the girls, so I'm safe. I know I can trust you, Diary.

Anyway, BIG YAWNS!

Must go to sleep now. Off to Dad's early tomorrow, just for the day.

Sunday 17th June

Dear Diary,

Back home now. Bet you feel like I was never gone.

So, another big announcement today from Dad and Eve. They've fixed a wedding date. It's been booked for a while, but they hadn't plucked up the courage to tell us until now. Think they were a bit scared after Nat's reaction to their engagement. But, funnily enough, Nat was fine about it. They're getting married on Friday 21st of December. A Christmas Wedding! I've always wanted to go to one of those.

It's going to be in a stately home called Branstone Manor, about ten miles away in the countryside. Eve says that it's going to be decorated 'all Christmassy.' She tentatively suggested that she'd like Nat and I to be her bridesmaids. That made us very excited. Nat seems to have forgotten all about not wanting Dad to marry anyone but Mum. She wanted to know all about what we would wear and how we would do our hair. Eve showed us some designs she had been sketching for the dresses. She said her friend Sienna, who's a dressmaker, and also going to be her chief bridesmaid, had agreed to make them. Dad was pleased at our enthusiasm, but did add a word of caution.

'Hang on a minute, you three. Remember we do have to get your mum's and school's permission, especially since it will be the last day of term.'

'Do you think she might make a fuss, Dad?' I asked. 'Because she can't really stop us, can she?'

'I hope not,' he said.

So, Eve really is going to be my stepmother in December. I'm glad. I like her and Nat gets on really well with her. I can't believe she's got no kids. She's good with Nat. But I guess she's young; there's plenty of time to have kids. There's a thought. I could have another sister, or a brother.

OOOH!

I messaged Zoe earlier to tell her the news. Of course, I might have known what she'd say.

Zoe: Zantabulous! She will be your wicked stepmother 4 real!

Me: IKR

Zoe: Now U'll have to watch out cos this is where it could all go horribly wrong. Mwah hah hah! 😁

Me: Shut up!

Zoe: LOL xx

Monday 18th June

Nat was really keen to ask Mum about us being bridesmaids. She wanted to do it last night, but I persuaded her to wait. If I'd made her wait any longer than tonight though, I think she would've exploded!

When we told her the wedding date and asked her about having the day off school and being bridesmaids, Mum wasn't very co-operative. She sighed, closed her eyes, rubbed her hands over her face and went to sit down in an armchair. We waited. She sat there frowning and thinking. To fill the awkward silence, Nat started to go on about the dresses and how cool they were and that they would be specially made, designed by Eve herself. I think that only made it worse. I kept giving Nat the 'shut up' look, but she wasn't taking any notice.

'Well Mum, can we, please?' I finally asked, when Nat had stopped talking.

'Oh, I don't know. What about school? It's the last day of term. Won't you have parties and plays and things?'

'Not on the last day,' Nat said. 'We don't do anything useful on the last day, just tidying up and watching movies. It's pretty boring.'

'Me neither. Waste of time being there,' I said, even though the last day could be quite a laugh.

'Well, I'm not paying for the dresses. If she's having them custom made, they'll cost a fortune!'

'I'm sure Dad wouldn't ask you to pay anything for

them, Mum,' I said.

'Huh, it must be costing Dad a fortune! Stately home, designer dresses!'

'You could come and see us doing our part, Mum. You'd love our dresses,' Nat enthused.

We both stared at her and she realised her mistake. She blushed.

'Please let us do it,' I begged.

'I'll think about it,' was all Mum would say.

'Please, please, please,' Nat begged, getting down on her knees and putting her hands together, making puppy-dog eyes at Mum. The she started whining like a little puppy too!

She looked so funny that I was about to burst out laughing, when Mum suddenly shouted, 'Just leave it, Natalie!' and stormed off upstairs.

Nat nearly cried. Mum can be so unreasonable sometimes! I told Nat not to mention it to Mum again for a while. I reckon Dad needs to sort this one out, but Mum needs time to calm down. Hope we haven't blown it.

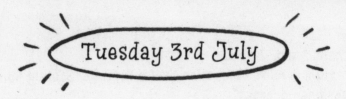

Tuesday 3rd July

Oops! Ages since I wrote to you, Diary. Sorry about that. Update time.

At school, I've been keeping Zoe informed about the wedding plans. She thinks the dresses sound gorgeous. Eve's is going to be very simple: White, sleeveless and clingy with a small train. She's going to have a tiara and a white cloak with fur trim too. (Fake of course!) Our dresses, presuming Mum relents (she hasn't yet, I'll come on to that!), are going to be apple-red and full length, with very thin straps and silver embroidery on the bodice. Eve says my black hair will look stunning with red. We're going to have gloves that come over our elbows, dainty shoes to match our dresses and white stoles to throw round our shoulders. We'll also have diamante headbands. Eve's going to get me a diamante nose stud to match hers. She showed us the designs she and Siena are working on. I posted pics to show everyone on Instagram. The room is going to be decorated with candles and holly. There'll be white and red roses and an enormous Christmas tree in the entrance hall. We're going to sing Christmas Carols too. Then, there's going to be a Christmas disco after all the speeches. Dad and Eve said we can make speeches too, if we want.

Zoe was spell-bound when I told her. 'It

sounds so magical. Can I come?'

'Hey, maybe you could. I'll ask Eve. I hope it snows.'

'Yeah! I hope Eve says yes. I'd love to be there and to finally meet the wicked stepmother!'

I gave her a shove.

'It would be pretty mean if your mum didn't let you do it,' Zoe added, reminding me of the real situation.

'I know. I really hope she lets us.'

'She's jealous of Eve,' Zoe said.

Despite how annoyed I was with Mum for holding back her answer for so long, I found myself defending her. 'She's not! Don't be stupid! It's just all happening so soon. It's hard for her. But she'd better say we can do it soon, or we'll be doing it anyway and she won't stop us.'

Dad has been really cross with Mum and so has Eve, although she has tried not to be mean about her in front of us. I heard her and Dad talking about it, and they were both annoyed. Eve gave Dad a kind of ultimatum (good word) and told him if he didn't sort it out in the next week, she was going to come round our house and tell Mum that we were going to be bridesmaids, whatever Mum said. Dad doesn't want any trouble, so he said he'd have a word.

On Sunday, when he dropped us off, he came in and asked Mum to let us do it. Nat and I were listening from the hallway. Mum was being obstinate (another of my good words), trying to make as many excuses as she could think of. Dad was trying to keep calm, but there was that edge in his voice. In the end, we couldn't stand it any longer and we burst into the room. Nat said she would be really, really, really (a hundred times) upset if Mum didn't let us be bridesmaids. I tried my best to persuade Mum.

Dad said, 'Remember what happened last time we didn't listen to them, Linda.'

She shot him a stony glare, then looked at our pleading faces and said, 'Alright. You can do it.'

Nat and I whooped with joy and danced around the living room, holding hands like we were three years old. Then Nat gave Mum a big hug and kiss. I joined in. Dad was smiling. Mum was looking grumpy, but when Nat started slobbering over her, like a puppy. She started laughing and the horrible atmosphere was broken.

Dad texted me later to say Eve was so happy and to tell Mum that they both appreciate her co-operation. I'm not sure I'd call it that!

Tuesday 10th July

Dear Diary,

Been quite concerned about Mum over the last couple of weeks. She's been quieter since the wedding announcement. She's been going to work, but when she gets home she doesn't say much. She's not asking Nat and I lots of questions about school. I've been making Nat's pack-ups and getting her up for school. It's like all the life has been sucked out of Mum. I've been wondering what to do about it. I have talked to Zoe, but she doesn't know what to do either. I don't think Dad could help. Mum would see it as interfering.

Today Miss Lowe (my form tutor, remember?) stopped me, as everyone was leaving for lessons. She wanted to know if I was okay.

Automatically I said yes.

'I've noticed you've been really quiet in form for the past week or so. Is everything alright at home?'

My stomach flipped. This was my inroad to tell someone about Mum. Handed to me on a plate. I chewed my lip. How should I start? What should I say? What if she got Social Services involved? So many questions bombarded my brain within a few seconds.

'I'm fine Miss,' I said. 'I'd better go. I'm gonna be late for geography.'

Miss Lowe smiled as I bolted for the door. 'If there's ever anything you want to talk about Lou...'

'Thanks Miss,' I said over my shoulder.

My heart was pounding as I hurried down the corridor to my lesson. Miss Lowe was nice. I should have told her. But I'm scared. And what could she do anyway?

*

Tonight, I tried to talk to Mum, a bit like Miss Lowe had tried with me. Mum was making tea. I wandered into the kitchen as casually as I could, but again, my heart was thudding so hard, I was sure she would have heard it, had it not been for all the pans clashing and water running. I tried to sound casual.

'Hi Mum. Have you had a good day?'

'Not bad. You?'

'It was okay.'

What to say next? It was really hard to bring the conversation round to what I wanted to talk about.

'Mum?'

'Yes.'

'Are you feeling okay?'

'Yes love. I'm fine.'

Clearly a lie! Try a different approach.

'Mum?'

'Yes.'

'I've noticed you being a bit quiet recently. And... sort of not really here.'

She turned round from chopping carrots and gave me a quizzical look. I gave her one back. There was a pause as she must have been deciding whether to tell me how she was really feeling, or just try harder to hide it. She came over to me and put her arm round me.

'Don't worry about me, love. I'm fine. Just been feeling a bit down lately. I'll get over it.' She squeezed me and went back to her chopping. As if to convince me she was fine, she started to hum. I wasn't convinced. She hadn't reassured me with that one-liner cover-up, but I wasn't sure how to pursue it. I came back to my room, but I'm still worried about her.

Tuesday 17th July

Dear Diary,

It's 7.30 a.m. but I just had to say...

End of term today.

Yipeeeeeeeeee!

Saturday 21st July

Dear Diary,

We've come to stay at Dad's for five days. It's the longest we've ever stayed here. We've been looking forward to it because we're not going on holiday this year. Mum says she can't afford it and Dad and Eve are saving for the wedding. Dad has promised us some good days out, visiting places. We really like our new bedroom here as well, even though we have to share. It's not so bad and we still love admiring all our work on the mural.

We didn't do much today, except go for the first fitting of our bridesmaid dresses. Eve said she hopes we don't grow too much between now and the wedding, but if we do, Siena can alter them. Siena is so cool. She wears her long hair in dreadlocks and has dyed it red. She wears big dangly earrings and chunky necklaces and bangles. She made us laugh a lot. The dresses are so gorgeous. I was messaging Zoe and sending her pics. She is so jealous.

Zoe: Zippidy-zoodlez! They are going to be amazing! Have U asked if I can come yet?
Me: Forgot
Zoe: Ask then

So, I asked Eve and she said she didn't have a problem

with it, but she'd have to check with Dad. Nat (of course) wanted her friend to come as well. When we talked to Dad about it, he said yes too!
YAY!

Me: You can come! 😁
Zoe: Yeeeehah! 😊 😊 😊 Better start planning what to wear! 😎
Me: It's not til December
Zoe: IK. Big decisions to make. Shoes, jewellery, outfit, matching bag ... Never been to a Christmas wedding
Me: Me neither. Sooooo excited! 😁 😁

Dear Diary,

Back home now. Had a good few days. Dad took time off work and took us to loads of places. We went to the cinema, ice-skating, the beach, visiting a castle (Dad's choice). It was good though, spending all that time with Dad. He can be really funny, if a bit embarrassing at times. Like when we went to this castle. He insisted on dressing up in the costumes area. Nat was up for it, but I declined! Dad dressed in a knight's costume and proceeded to charge around pretending he was on a horse and slaying dragons! It was very funny, but I kept my distance in case anyone thought he was with me. Nat was in fits of giggles. I filmed it on my phone to show my friends.

Eve didn't come out with us much, apart from Sunday, which was a bit disappointing. She said she had a work deadline that she had to concentrate on. So, we didn't see much of her after the weekend. But it was a good opportunity to have Dad all to ourselves.

Big surprise when we got home. Mum announced that she has booked us a last-minute holiday! She got a cheap deal on a

week in Spain. We're flying to Alicante on Saturday!!!!!
Soooooo excited!

Must do some shopping for strappy tops, bikini, shorts. Mum says she can afford to buy us a few new things to go away. I asked her if I could go by myself (with Zoe) to buy my stuff. She's just about got over the 'incident' with the hair and piercings now. She gave me a warning look, but then said yes. She was actually smiling for the first time in ages, so maybe this holiday will do her the world of good too.

I messaged Zoe:

Me: guess what? Mum's got us a holiday. Going to Spain THIS SATURDAY!
Zoe: Zoweeee! Lucky U
Me: Can you come shopping with me tomorrow?
Zoe: Yeah. K. Need some stuff for my holiday too
Me: Where U going?
Zoe: The caravan
Me: That'll be good
Zoe. Suppose so 😐

Poor Zoe. She goes to the same place every year with her family. Rick's dad owns the caravan site so they get a caravan really cheap.

Thursday 26th July

Dear Diary,

BIG SHOCK today and don't know what to do about it. Here's what happened...

I met Zoe at McDonalds in town and had lunch, then we went looking for clothes. We both got some cool stuff and were having a great time trying things on. Then, we were walking up the high street when I spotted Eve up ahead in Redmayne Square.

I said to Zoe, 'Hey, there's Eve. Do you want to go say hello?'

Of course, Zoe was up for it. She's been dying to meet Eve for ages and stopped calling her Evil Eve month ago. We walked a bit faster to try and catch her up and just as we got close enough for me to shout her name, a young, hot guy walked up to her. They smiled at each other, then hugged for ages, then...

THEY KISSED!

Not a big snog or anything, cos this was in the middle of the street. Just on the cheek, but still! I grabbed Zoe's arm and we stopped in our tracks! She looked at me and I looked at her as if we'd seen a ghost!

She said something stupid like, 'That's not your dad!'

'Duh! I know that!'

They went into this café called Latte-dah.

'What shall we do?' I said.

'We should follow them. See what they get up to,'

Zoe said.

We walked on the other side of the street and tried to see them through the café windows. We couldn't see them anywhere, but the place was crowded. There were some tables outside, but they weren't full, as it wasn't a very warm day.

'Let's go in,' Zoe said.

'No! What if she sees us! That would be totally awkward!' I said.

'Come on,' Zoe insisted. 'you need to know if she's cheating on your dad.'

'It looks that way to me already,' I said.

'We need more evidence!' Zoe said, dragging me towards the café door.

Just then, the door opened and out came Eve and the Hot Guy, carrying a tray.

'Quick!' I hissed. We ducked behind a row of bins and I peered round the edge. They were sat opposite each other, at a table, drinking coffee. Zoe peered over the top of the bins. We couldn't hear what they were talking about, but they were laughing.

'Look! She's touching his arm,' I almost screeched.

'Calm down!' Zoe said. 'She'll hear you if you get any louder!'

We kept watching, but it was so frustrating not being able to hear. They kept touching arms and hands. I couldn't believe she was flirting with this guy when she was engaged to my dad and going to get married soon. I had visions of the whole wedding being called off and dad crying on his own in the house! I was getting really mad.

'I wish we could hear what they're saying!' I said.

Then Zoe had an idea. 'Eve doesn't know what I look like. I could wander over there and pretend I'm looking in the window. See what I can hear.'

'Go on then, I said. But don't say anything to them!'

She walked casually over to the café and proceeded to peer into the window as if she was looking for someone. She stood a few tables away from Eve and Hot Guy, but she was being a bit over the top. I could see her peering in the window, then sighing, looking at her watch (that she wasn't wearing!), turning round, peering exaggeratedly down the street, turning round, staring at Eve. My heart was in my mouth, thinking she was going to make them suspicious. But they were too wrapped up in each other to notice her. After a few minutes, Eve stood up. Hot Guy went back into the café. When he came out, they hugged again for ages and he kissed her again, then they went their separate ways. Hot Guy was coming towards the bins. I scrambled up and shot off in the other direction.

I stood outside Boots and motioned to Zoe to come over. 'What were they talking about?'

'I didn't catch it all,' she said, 'But she was telling him about her Mum and Dad and other trivial stuff.'

'Did she mention me and Nat, or Dad?'

'No,' Zoe said. 'I heard him say he'd really missed her and had forgotten how brilliant she was!'

Oh my goodness! Now I got it. She was getting back with an ex-boyfriend. I felt tears start to sting my eyes. She must have got bored with my dad and gone back to Hot Guy. I mean, he was so good-looking and much younger than my dad, I almost couldn't blame her. But then she shouldn't have hooked up with my dad in the first place. And she certainly shouldn't have got engaged to him. Nat will be devastated.

Zoe asked me what I was going to do. I shrugged, because I thought if I spoke I'd end up crying in the street and didn't want that.

I've been messaging Zoe tonight. She thinks I shouldn't do anything 'til we come back from Spain. I think she's right. It will give me time to think. I hope it doesn't spoil my whole holiday though.

Saturday 28th July

~~~~~~~~~~~~~~~~~~~~~~~~~~~~

4am setting off to the airport.

Bleugh!

See you in Spain, Diary.

We arrived at the hotel about midday. It's lovely. The room is quite nice: A bit squashed cos we're all in the same room, but that doesn't matter as we'll be outside most of the time. The hotel has two big pools, a bar with entertainment in the evenings, and wifi in the bar area.

YAY!

So, I can keep in touch with my friends and send them pics of the place.

As soon as we'd dumped our stuff, we came down to the pool. I'm just sunning myself and writing to you Dear Diary. It's already crowded, but we managed to grab two loungers. Mum is reading, next to me, and seems really chilled out and Nat is in the pool already. It's going to be a good week. I had managed to put Eve to the back of my mind while I was getting ready to come on holiday, but I've just read again what happened on Thursday. I need to distract myself. I'm going in the pool.

Monday 30th July

Hi Diary,

It's been really cool here so far. (Ha! Which is funny, cos the weather has been hot, hot, hot!) The food is very yummy too. All Nat wants to do is play in the pool, but today, we went to a Theme Park called Terra Mitica. It had loads of crazy rides. Mum loves that kind of thing and we had a great time together. It was brilliant to see her laughing her head off and acting like a big kid again. She bought us all a cuddly animal each, in the shop. We gave them funny names and called them the three amigos (Spanish for friends). Mine was a giraffe that I called Leggy (I know, original), Nat's was a snake that she called Squiggles and Mum's was a lion cub that she called Leonard.

It did make me think of the fairground fiasco we had with Dad and Eve, earlier in the year. I've been messaging Zoe (in her caravan, poor Zoe). She's been calling her Evil Eve again since last Thursday. Anyway, trying not to think about it. Just enjoy myself.

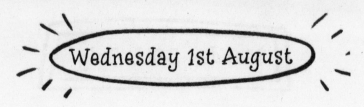

Wednesday 1st August

Hi again, Diary,

Want to know what we did today? What about yesterday? Okay, well quickly then... we just stayed by the pool for most of yesterday, then we went and did some shopping for souvenirs at the local touristy craft market. I got some nice bangles and earrings. Nat got a hair braid and we both got temporary dolphin tattoos.
Now for today:

The BEST DAY EVER!

Knowing how much we love dolphins, Mum had arranged a really cool surprise. We went to this water park where you can actually swim with dolphins!

LOUD EXCITED SQUEALS!

You can imagine what Nat and I were like. We had an amazing time. There was a small group of us in the water with two dolphins, called Dante and Damita. We wore snorkels and got to swim beside them, stroke them and hold onto their fins while they pulled us along. Mum took loads of photos. I made her use my phone too, so I could show my friends when I got back to the hotel. It was Dolphintastic!
I got loads of messages back after I posted the pics.

I think everyone was jealous. Felt a bit mean to Zoe (in her caravan), if I'm totally honest, but I couldn't not share those pics, could I? I thought of sending one to Dad, but then I couldn't face talking to him, so I decided not to.

Gave Mum the biggest hugs ever, after that. She was really pleased.

A-MAZ-ING!

Mum is the BEST!

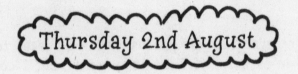

Thursday 2nd August

We went to the beach today. It was too hot and crowded and we didn't enjoy it much, so we came back to the pool. Not much else to tell.

Going home tomorrow.

Boooo!

Not been worrying about Dad and Eve.

No. No. No. Definitely not!

Friday 3rd August

Dear Diary,

Last day today. Boooo!

We managed to spend the morning in the pool, but had to vacate our room by ten, so had to get dried in the changing rooms by the pool and keep our suitcases behind reception.

Now we're sitting in the airport. Why do you have to get here two hours before the flight? It's so boring. Nothing much to do, once you've looked round the duty free and had a burger. I've had a fab holiday though. And Mum's been back to her old self, which has been great. I'm starting to get worried about going to Dad's though. We're supposed to be going next weekend. I don't want to go. I mean, what will I say to Eve? I just don't want to be around them, acting like a happy family and me knowing that it's all going to be blown to pieces when Dad finds out she's seeing Hot Guy behind his back. I should say something, but how would I prove it? Should have taken photos. Why didn't I think of that at the time? I'm surprised Zoe didn't.

I might have to fake illness next weekend and tell Mum I'd rather stay at home. Got to get on the plane now. They're calling our flight and Mum's hassling me.

Zoe came round today. Mum is back at work and Nat's gone to a friend's, but Mum said Zoe and I could stay here by ourselves, as long as we were sensible. She gave me that stern look and told me to call her, if necessary.

Zoe was really keen to see all my pics. I thought she might not be interested, but she's not the kind to hold a grudge. I asked her lots of questions about her holiday too, but she said it rained and it did sound quite boring, to be honest.

Then she got onto the subject of Dad and Eve and Hot Guy, as we're calling him.

'You should try and find out what's going on Lou, otherwise your life is going to be so awkward every time you go round there. My dad had lots of different girlfriends after he split with Mum. I lost count in the end. Some people just can't make up their minds.'

'I know,' I said, 'But I didn't think Eve was like that.'

'Ah, you just never know,' she said, sounding like a wise old owl. 'Under the surface of nice Eve there lies...'

Here, she paused for dramatic effect, made a horrible face and witchy claws, 'EVIL EVE! Mwah-hah-hah!'

I couldn't help laughing, but said, 'It's not funny,

really. I'm not going on Saturday. I can't.'

She said I should go and ask her about Hot Guy to her face. I don't think I could do that.

'Well at least go and see if she's behaving differently around your dad.'

'Like how?' I asked.

'You know, faking it. Being *tooooo* nice to him and you and Nat. Or being moody and saying horrible things to you.'

I shrugged.

Zoe hugged me. 'Cheer up. We'll think of something.'

A while later, she suddenly said, 'I know. You should show her the photo I took of her and Hot Guy at the table.'

I looked at her in amazement. 'You got a picture and you didn't think to tell me?'

'I forgot. It was kind of panicky at the end, then they got up to leave and then you went on holiday.'

'Let me see it,' I said.

She got her phone out and scrolled through her pictures. 'Here.'

I snatched the phone out of her hand and stared at it.

'It's a bit blurry because I was taking it from under my bags.'

'I didn't even see you take it,' I said.

'That's because I'm a good spy,' she said.

The picture showed Eve and Hot Guy, sitting at the table. They didn't look as if they were doing anything wrong. She wasn't touching his arm at that point, or anything.

I frowned. 'This doesn't prove anything. They're not doing anything! He could just be a friend.'

Zoe shrugged. 'I tried. Maybe you could show it to her and challenger her, like, Hey, me and Zoe saw you with him. Who is he then? We saw you kissing and hugging him and flirting with him!'

I thought about it. That might be an idea. Zoe messaged me the evidence so I could challenge her, but I didn't think I could do it. Zoe could, of course. If only she could come with me.

Saturday 11th August

Dear Diary,

I've tried to fake illness, but the fateful day has arrived. Mum is going to visit Grandma for a couple of days and she says that even if I'm not very well I can still go to Dad's and he'll look after me. I tried hard to get her to let me come to Grandma's with her, but she seems to want to go on her own. Dad will be here in half an hour. Nat is all excited. She can't wait to tell him and Eve about Spain. She wants to show them all the pictures on my phone, but I don't want Evil Eve to see them.

*

Hi again. It's Saturday night. Dad, Eve and Nat are downstairs watching a movie. I couldn't stand it. I think it must all be an act, all this nicey-nicey family stuff. I had to let her see the pictures of the holiday, because Nat was so insistent. Eve asked me if everything was alright at one point this afternoon. I felt like shouting in her face,

'No! And you know why!'

But I didn't. she thought I was still not feeling well. At least it was a good excuse to come up to our room and be away from them. I can't stand it, if every weekend with them is going to be like this. And more importantly I can't let Dad marry her.

Zoe: Have U showed her the pic yet?
Me: No
Zoe: Y not?
Me: Can't
Zoe: U have 2
Me: Scared
Zoe: Show her. You've got 2 know
Me: 😨

Monday 13th August

Went to the cinema with Zoe, Meg and Alice today. Good film. Zoe kept whispering to me about Dad and Eve though. I didn't want to think about it, but she can't drop it. She's like a detective on a murder enquiry, she has to solve it.

'You should try and get hold of her phone, next time you're there. See if there's any incriminating evidence on it.'

'Like what?' I asked.

'Zounds! You are so naïve girl!' she said. 'Like pictures of them together, texts, messages. Duh!'

'I dunno. What if she caught me?'

'Well, make sure she doesn't. Then you'd have evidence to show your dad. And she couldn't wriggle out of it then.'

'She wouldn't keep stuff about him on her phone,' I said. 'That would be stupid.'

'Yeah, people are stupid,' Zoe said, like she knows these things.

'I dunno,' I said again. Then we got told to shhhh by the people in front of us, so that was the end of that.

I might ask Dad if Zoe can come over next weekend when we're there again. She could do some snooping and maybe help me confront Eve. I just don't know what to do!

Wednesday 15th August

I texted Dad, to ask about Zoe, but he said we had a busy weekend and maybe she could come another time.

Oh great!!!

Saturday 18th August

Dear Diary,

I was feeling physically sick today as Dad came to pick us up, but I didn't dare say I was ill two weekends in a row. Mum would get suspicious and that would worry her more. She's gone quiet again since getting back from holiday and I don't want to make things worse. I have decided to talk to Dad though. Maybe not say Eve's cheating on him just yet, but ask him if he is still sure he wants to marry her. Maybe he's having doubts and I could persuade him not to marry her after all. I'm glad I can confide in you, Dear Diary.

*

Just heard him ring the doorbell so I'd better go.

So now it's about 11p.m. and Nat is asleep. I can fill you in on what happened earlier.

Eve and Nat seem to get on really well these days and I keep thinking that she's just a bit over the top when Dad's around. She took Nat to this big indoor play place for the afternoon because it was raining. I said I wasn't feeling too good so Dad and I stayed here. This was my chance to talk to him. I was playing on my phone and he was watching sport on TV. All the time I could hear Zoe, in my head, cackling like a wicked stepmother, saying, 'Go on! Talk to him!'

'Dad?' I said, not looking up from my phone.

'Yes,' He said, not looking away from the TV.

'Do you still think you want to get married to Eve?' I sneaked a glance.

'That's a funny thing to say. Yes, of course,' he said, still looking at the TV.

'I just wondered if you might be having second thoughts. Maybe thinking it's too soon after you and Mum split up.'

'No, I don't think so,' he said.

'Getting married is quite old-fashioned isn't it? Maybe you want to be more modern,' I suggested.

He paused the TV and looked at me. 'We're looking forward to getting married Lou. What's up? I thought you were looking forward to the wedding.'

'I am. I just thought you might be having second thoughts,' I said, furiously pretending to concentrate on my game, but not really.

'No, why would I be?'

This was my big moment to say, 'because Evil Eve is seeing some Hot Guy behind your back.' Instead, I said, 'Don't you think you're a bit old for Eve? Maybe?'

He laughed. 'Oh. You think she's too young for me? Am I that much of an old man eh?'

'No, not really, it's just...'

He interrupted me. 'Age doesn't matter when you're an adult, Lou. Lots of people with big age differences get married.'

'I know,' I said. This wasn't going very well. 'Never mind.'

'Don't worry about it, love,' he said, hitting the play

button again, 'We're very well suited. We'll be fine. You'll see.'

I wanted to blurt it all out. I wanted to shout at him and tell him that things don't always work out FINE! We are not in a fairy tale!

*

Eve and Nat came back later, laughing and joking. Nat was eating sweets. She told me what a great time she'd had and that they'd bumped into her friend, Sophie, from school.

We ate pizza and watched TV. I couldn't really slope off to my room again. Everything was *sooooo cosy!*

Wednesday 22nd August

Dear Diary,

I've been with Zoe all day. And what a day! We went into town. I couldn't help being on the look-out for Eve and Hot Guy, but we didn't see them. We went to a coffee shop for a smoothie.

'Right,' Zoe said. 'This can't go on. You're a wreck! We have to have it out with Eve.'

'I can't,' I whined.

'Yes, we can,' she said. 'You know your dad's address. Your dad will be at work, right? You and me are going round there now. We show her the picture on your phone and ask her to explain who he is!'

'No, I couldn't.'

'We have to, Lou.'

'She could lie,' I said.

'We know the truth,' Zoe said.

'Well, we don't actually know...'

She cut me off. 'Stop making excuses. Come on. I'll do the talking.'

Most of me didn't want to do this. Most of me hoped she would be out. But part of me did want to find out the truth, whatever the consequences. Dad deserved to know.

We got on the number twelve bus that goes

past Dad's house. Honestly, I've never felt so queasy on a bus, even that time I sat upstairs at the back with Mum and Nat. I was getting all sweaty and hot. Zoe, meanwhile was listening to music, one earphone in her ear, talking to me about random things.

We arrived outside Dad and Eve's house.

'I can't,' I said, pathetically one more time.

Zoe grabbed my arm. 'Shut up! Come on.' She rang the bell.

'She's not in,' I said after a few seconds.

'Wait.' Zoe gripped my arm more firmly. She rang again. Then we heard footsteps coming up the hallway.

We both gasped as the door opened.

It was HIM. Hot Guy! In my dad's house!

We stood there mouths hanging open, like two dummies.

'Can I help you ladies?' he asked from his wide-grinning, perfect-teeth mouth.

We still gawped.

Then came Eve's voice from the living room, 'Who is it, Shaun?'

He shouted back. 'It's two young ladies who seem to have lost the power of speech!'

At that point, Eve came to the door.

'Oh!' She looked surprised, but quickly faked a smile. 'Hi Lou and… friend. This is an unexpected visit.'

We still said nothing.

'Would you like to come in?'

I thought it might get ugly if we did this on the

street, so we followed her and Hot Guy (or should I say Shaun) into the room.

'Can I get you a drink?' she said, as Zoe and I sat on the sofa, opposite the daisy-chain girl.

Somehow, I managed to speak. 'No thanks.' (Still remember my manners, even in time of crisis.)

'So, to what do we owe this pleasure? Your dad's at work.'

Of course he is, I thought, if *he's* here.

'We've come to find out who he is?' Zoe piped up, pointing at Shaun.

They looked quizzically at each other.

'Have you?' Eve said. 'But you've never met him before.'

'Ah, but we've seen you two together.' Zoe was gaining confidence now. 'We saw you at the Latte-dah café a few weeks ago. You were hugging and you kissed.'

Zoe got her phone out and found the picture. I didn't know where to look. I felt like my face was on fire. She showed the picture to Eve, who reached out to take the phone. 'No!' Zoe said. 'You can't hold it. You might delete the evidence!'

I expected Eve to start shouting at us to get out or something. I was nearly in tears. But, to my surprise Eve smiled.

'Not the best picture of us, Shaun,' she said, pulling him closer to take a look. He looked a bit worried and glanced nervously at us. Zoe pulled her phone back and put it in her pocket.

Eve said, 'Shaun, this is Mike's daughter, Lou. And

this, I'm guessing, is her best friend, Zoe.'

Shaun smiled but didn't show his perfect-teeth this time. 'Hi,' he said and gave a sheepish wave. 'Nice to meet you... I think.'

Nice to meet us? Was he serious?

Eve was stopped smiling. 'So, you've been spying on me, Lou?' She looked directly at me.

I didn't know how to start, but I had to say something now. 'I... well... it was just by chance that we saw you. But then when we saw you kissing and hugging and... well... flirting with each other at the table, we had to find out what's going on.'

Eve nodded. 'That's why you've been acting a bit odd around me lately, isn't it?'

'Yes,' I said, feeling my nerves morphing into anger. 'What do you expect me to feel if I see you cheating on my dad? It's been driving me mad, having to be here and knowing that he doesn't know, and not knowing what to do about it. Then Zoe said we should come here, and I didn't want to, but now we're here, and you know that we know, and I think my dad should know the truth, and if you don't tell him, I will, so what are you going to do?'

Phew!

That was a long ramble, but I'd got it out!

Eve raised her eyebrows. She looked at Shaun, who looked like he was trying to hold back a laugh. How dare he!

'Hmmmm,' she said. 'Let me see...'

Shaun spoke then. 'Eve. Stop dragging this out. You're

being mean. Tell them who I am.'

Eve burst out laughing.

'It's not funny!' Zoe shouted. I thought she was going to punch her!

Eve shook her head. 'No, you're absolutely right, Zoe. It's not. Girls, let me introduce you to Shaun. Shaun is my long lost brother. He's been travelling in Australia for the last year and he came home a few weeks ago. He's been staying at our parents', and yesterday he moved in here for a while, until he can rent a flat. Your dad and I were keeping it a surprise, to introduce you and Nat to him, next time you came.'

Again, Zoe and I were speechless. This was her brother? Could she be lying? But if she was, it was a stupid lie, because she just told us he was living here now. I felt like a complete idiot and just wanted to run away right now, but my bum wouldn't move from the sofa.

Shaun smiled again and held out a hand to us. 'Pleased to meet you both.'

We shook hands automatically.

'Sorry to keep you dangling like that,' Eve said. 'I couldn't resist it when you'd done all that detective work. Nice to finally meet you, Zoe. You're a good friend to Lou. I can see that. Loyal and brave. I like you already.'

Zoe recovered quite easily from this second shock. 'Thanks. Nice to meet you too. I've been wanting to for ages.'

Eve made us some drinks then, and brought out some

of her home-made cakes. She and Shaun did their best to make us laugh and cheer me up. I couldn't stop feeling stupid. Shaun seemed so nice. He told us loads about his Australia trip. Zoe was loving every minute of it.

When we had to go, Eve put her arm round me and said, 'Don't worry, Lou. No hard feelings. And I won't tell your dad, unless you make me mad, of course, then I might take my revenge!' She did a wicked stepmother laugh. 'It can be our little secret to laugh about in years to come!'

*

What a day! Now I'm writing it all down for you, Diary, I feel totally relieved that I know the truth and it's not what I'd dreaded.

Just got a message from Zoe.

> Zoe: Zowee! What a guy! You're so lucky. He's going to be your step-uncle!
>
> Me: 😶

Sunday 2nd September

Dear Diary,

We didn't go to Dad's last weekend, as Mum wanted us to go to Grandma's, which was slightly boring. At least she has Wi-Fi!

Yesterday, we came to Dad's for the weekend. I was dreading it a little bit, because I knew Shaun would be there and I had to keep it to myself all this time. Nat was going to get a surprise and I would have to fake it.

I think I did a good job. He winked at me, (both in on the big secret) when no one else was looking, which was cool. I did have to listen to all the Australia stories all afternoon, and look at all his photos again, but I didn't mind. Small price to pay for keeping the secret.

Nat is now totally besotted with him. He made us laugh all weekend and did stuff with us. We went over to the park and she made Shaun push her on the swing, hold her hand across the road, be on her team to play football, help her on the climbing frame... Poor Dad! I think he felt a bit left out! I made sure I talked to him and chose him to be on my team.

It wasn't too bad with Eve. She never mentioned the incident in front of the others. The only thing that was a bit awkward was, when we were alone in the kitchen, she did say to me she hoped I wouldn't feel the need to snoop on her ever again. I was a bit surprised at that, but I said no, of course not. I wanted to say that we hadn't been snooping, we just saw them by accident, but then we had snooped, so I thought best not to go on about it. She said she hoped I would trust her from now on. I said yes again. Apart from that, it got easier as the weekend went on. She didn't treat me any differently than normal and we had a few laughs too. I feel like I can breathe again now.

When we got home tonight. Nat insisted on telling Mum all about 'uncle Shaun' as she called him. She went on and on and on. I could tell Mum wasn't really interested and didn't want to know. She did say, at one point, 'He's not really your uncle you know,' (which I thought was a bit mean) but Nat just said, 'He will be soon though, when Dad and Eve get married.' Mum didn't reply. I tried to steer Nat into another conversation about getting ready for school, but it didn't work. I think Mum just switched off and let Nat talk herself out.

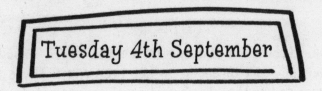

Tuesday 4th September

Back to school today.
Year Nine!

Eeeeeeek!

Friday 28th September

Poor old Diary! I've not let you know anything for ages. To be honest, not much has been going on worth writing about. The only thing is, Mum has been odd again. You know how before we went on holiday, she was all quiet and 'can't be bothered.' Well, she's doing it again. She's not going out with friends, or laughing and joking. She's been making us meals and doing the washing and that kind of thing, but she doesn't talk much.

And tonight, I caught her crying in the bathroom. She tried to cover it up when I walked in on her, but this time I just asked her, out right, what was wrong. She wouldn't tell me. She just made some excuse about being tired and stuff. I decided to be bolder.

'Mum, I know you're not happy. What can I do to help?'

She was a bit taken aback at this.

'Honestly, I'll be fine Lou. It's not something I want you to worry about.'

'But I do worry, Mum,' I said. 'You can't hide it all from me. When I know you're secretly unhappy I can't help but worry.'

The tears started to well up in her eyes again. 'That's kind of you, love. There's not really anything you can do. I just need to work through some stuff in my own mind.'

I suggested that maybe Nat and I should spend a

weekend with her, instead of going to Dad's every weekend. She said that would be nice, but not this time, as it would be a bit short notice for Dad. So, I said I'd talk to him about us staying here next weekend. She seemed pleased at that, and gave me a hug.

Sunday 21st October

Dear Diary,

It's half term and we're staying at Dad's all week, 'til Friday, then having the weekend with Mum. Things have been slightly better with Mum, although she still seems sad. I think having us at home the other weekend really helped. She was more lively and the three of us went bowling together. This week, I persuaded her to go stay with her old friend, Melissa, from University, who she hasn't seen for ages. She's friends with her on Facebook, so I got in touch with Melissa and asked if I could surprise Mum by arranging for her to visit. Melissa was really pleased. So, Mum went off to Norwich yesterday. I can't work out if she was happy or not, but I'm sure she'll have a good time.

This week we've got lots of wedding stuff to do. Dress fittings, shoe shopping, accessories shopping. Eve's friend is making the cake to Eve's design. Zoe is coming over on Thursday and Dad says she can sleep over. She's dying to see Shaun again. She's always asking me questions about him at school. Here's what she messaged me the other night.

Zoe: Can't wait for Thursday to see the gorgeous Shaun again
Me: Shut up!
Zoe: MMMMM he's Zoelicious!

> Me: 😛
> Zoe: I've been dreaming about him
> Me: Urgh!

She sends me stuff like that all the time. Definitely got a crush on him! Poor Shaun! I dread to think what she'll be like on Thursday!

He's moving out next week. He's got a flat about ten miles away. At least that might stop Zoe going on about him. But he's coming to the wedding, so Nat is happy. And Zoe!

Saturday 27th October

We got back from Dad's last night. Mum actually came and picked us up on her way back from Norwich. (First time ever that she's come near Dad's house.)

It's been a great week. The dress fitting went well. They're almost done now. Just a few little tweaks needed here and there. Siena is coming to the wedding so she'll see her handiwork in action. She's made Eve's dress too, but no one has been allowed to see that yet. Top secret. The shopping was good. Got most of our sparkly bits and the shoes are so gorgeous. Not going to tell you about them until the big day though, Diary. Don't want to spoil all the surprises!

Zoe did not behave herself around Shaun. She was like a big daft puppy, bouncing around him. She'd have wagged her tail if she had one! I had to keep digging her in the ribs and telling her to calm down and shut up. She was being such a flirt. *Sooooo* embarrassing! I think she was getting on Eve's nerves, because I saw her giving Dad 'the look' and she did tell Zoe to leave Shaun alone a few times. Anyway, he did make it *very* clear to her that he has a girlfriend, which made her sulk for a few hours. So, she left him alone after that.

*

Today, I caught Nat telling Mum all about the bridesmaid dresses and the shopping and 'uncle Shaun,' in great detail. Mum was making an effort to be interested, but I marched in and changed the subject, abruptly. Then I suggested we go out for an autumn walk. Mum gave me the oddest look! Okay, walking is not my favourite thing, but Mum seemed to like the idea.

While we were out, I asked her about her stay with Melissa. She said she'd had a lovely time and was glad she went.

Phew!

Another good deed has paid off! Maybe she will be a bit happier now!

Hi Diary,

Just checking in with you. The weeks are dragging on and there's nothing much to tell you. I'm just wishing the time away 'til the wedding. We're so excited, but it's hard trying not to show it in front of Mum. When we go to Dad's it's fine and we get all buzzed up about it. But, I want to protect Mum. It's weird, isn't it? Parents are supposed to protect us, but sometimes it turns around. Mum's been okay the past few weeks: A bit perkier, but still not right. I think it's helping that we don't go to Dad's every weekend now and we spend at least one with her every month.

Dad is fine with it. I overheard him and Eve talking in the kitchen last night and Eve was saying she likes her 'weekend off' and she wished she could have a few more weekends with just the two of them. I felt a bit upset when I heard that. Dad sort of agreed with her, then he added, 'but I have to get whatever time I can with the girls.' I'm not sure if that meant he felt it was his duty, or he just wanted to. Left me feeling a bit confused. I haven't told Nat. No point in upsetting her. I told Zoe though. This was our conversation.

Me: Hi
Zoe: ZUP?
Me: Eve

Zoe: UH OH! Being wicked?
Me: Kinda
Zoe: How?
Me: Just heard her say to Dad she would rather have more weekends 2 themselves
Zoe: Oh 🙁
Me: Yeah
Zoe: U could kind of expect that
Me: Why?
Zoe: They're just about 2 get married. They're in LUURRRVE!
Me: But it's been fine so far
Zoe: Weddings make people get more romantic.
Me: Oh 😖
Zoe: Don't worry. Will all be fine
Me: K
Zoe: *Hugs* XOXO
Me: THX XOXO

Good to talk to Zoe about it, but still felt sad.

Saturday 8th December

Hi Diary,

Today we went to Branstone Manor with Dad and Eve.

Wow!
That's all I'm saying.

I'm saving all the details for the big day. All of us girls got the giggles and were being really silly, because we were so excited. They showed us into the room where the service was going to be and, when no one was looking, Eve, Nat and I pretended we were in our dresses and floated down the aisle, with Eve singing
'Here comes the bride, big fat and wide.
Here comes the groom, skinny as a broom!'
Dad was going, 'Shhh, come on, we should get out of here.' But we were just laughing at him.
Dad bought us lunch in the posh restaurant. After that, he and Eve did get all serious and had to go off and have discussions with the manager about boring stuff. Nat and I just had to hang around playing on our phones.
Eve has always struck me as a laid-back kind of person. but after we left, she was quite stressed out. I think there was some issue about the reception. I've never really heard her snap at anyone (except that time with Zoe) but she was a bit snappy with all of us

tonight. She and Dad spent the evening wrestling with the guest list, arguing a bit over who was still coming and where to put some of them.

So, Nat and I just watched TV in the other room and turned up the volume.

Aaarrrgh!

Zoe is driving me nuts this week. You think I'm excited about the wedding? She is going mental. She has talked about nothing else all week: What she's wearing, who will be there, what I'm wearing, what Eve's wearing (top secret!), will there be any boys there, what songs will they play at the disco etc etc.

Aaarrrgh!

Anyway, only one week to go. Still managing to just about keep Nat from bursting with excitement at home with Mum, but she keeps coming into my room and talking to me about it. She's so cute though, I can't be cross with her.

I wonder if things will stay the same after Dad's married?

Friday 21st December

Hey there Diary,

Finally, the BIG DAY has arrived and I'm going to tell you every last detail of it! Our head teachers have allowed us the day off school. Our form tutor said we must bring in the photos after Christmas. Dad is picking Nat and I up at 9a.m. Our dresses are at his house. Mum has been very quiet all week; sulking I think. But I'm not going to let her make me feel guilty about enjoying today. Just heard the doorbell, so got to go. Catch you later...

*

So, it's all over. And I was too tired last night, so it's actually the next morning as I write this, but I'm not changing the date as it's all about yesterday. Confusing, eh, Diary? Sorry. Anyway, enough blah blah blah. Let's start from the moment I left off, as Dad came.

It felt strange as Dad came to the door. Mum didn't speak to him and avoided eye contact. She just gave us a kiss and a bigger hug than normal. All she could manage was 'Bye then.' She didn't even wish us luck on our big role as bridesmaids. I thought that was a bit off, especially for Nat. She closed the door and didn't even wave to us like she normally would. The excitement I had been feeling tripped over the guilt and fell flat on its face. But in the car, I told myself that it was her problem, not mine, and I was going to enjoy myself and not think about Mum all day!

Dad was determined to make sure the whole day was positive and happy. In the car, he laughed and joked and told us funny stories; like how Eve was petrified of having her dress tucked in her knickers as she walked down the aisle! And she had rehearsed 'I do' about a million times in the last week! He soon had us laughing and my excitement picked itself up.

Eve wasn't at the house. She had gone to stay with her Mum overnight. I wondered what the point of this was, when they had been living together for ages, but I suppose it's just tradition. There were a few hours to kill before we needed to get ready, as the ceremony wasn't starting until 4p.m. Eve wanted it to be getting dark outside. She'd said it would help create an atmosphere with the lighted candles. I wished it had snowed, that would have been awesome, but I didn't really expect it to, and, to be honest, I didn't mind as long as it didn't rain.

We got into our bridesmaid's dresses. Fortunately, Siena came round to help, otherwise goodness knows how we would have turned out, under Dad's supervision. Then a girl called Tina turned up. Eve had booked her to style our hair. Nat and I couldn't believe our eyes when we looked in the mirror and saw glamorous models staring back. Then Dad came in, dressed in his morning suit. He looked great, and very happy. Siena fussed over his collar and cuffs and patted his bottom a few times! (To smooth out creases she said!) Tina put some gel in his hair and spiked it up a bit. That made us laugh, but he did look quite cool when they'd finished. Finally, we were ready to go. There was no posh car to take us, but Dad had polished his car and put ribbons on it to make it look all weddingy!

We got to Branstone Manor before anyone else arrived. Dad had a few things to see to. His brother, Uncle Steve, had driven up from London, to be his best man, and he was waiting for Dad outside the front door. We chatted for a short while, but it was cold, so he took us inside and bought us a coke each, while he and Dad sorted things out.

The place was gorgeous. There was a huge Christmas tree in the entrance hall, reaching almost to the ceiling. It was beautifully decorated and already shimmering with tiny fairy lights, in the fading light. There were old-fashioned lanterns all around, waiting to be lit, and holly and ivy strewn everywhere. It was magical. Dad was soon back to escort us to the room where the ceremony was to take place.

'Everyone okay?' he asked, beaming nervously at us.

We nodded. The room was brilliantly decorated. There were lanterns and tea lights everywhere, mingled with all sorts of white and red flowers and lengths of

trailing ivy. Several of the hotel staff were in the process of lighting all the candles. Quite a few people were milling around now. We saw Dad's other brother, Mark, with Auntie Julie and our cousins. There were a few of Dad's friends that I recognised. And Shaun was there. He waved at us. I wondered if Eve's mum and dad were there? I just realised I'd never met them.

Then we saw Grandad. 'Aren't you the belles of the ball,' he chuckled, kissing us. He does have some funny, old-fashioned expressions!

Next, Zoe arrived. She spotted us and came straight over. 'You look Zamazing! The dresses look even better in real life than I'd imagined! And this place is so cool!'

'I know,' I said. 'Maybe I am in Cinderella after all!'

Of course, that set her off with her, 'Mwah hah hahs' and we both fell about in a giggling fit, until Nat told us off for creasing my dress. Oops! Sorry little sis!

Soon, most of the seats were full. The celebrant (person doing the ceremony) was ready at the front. She had a chat with Nat and I, making us feel more relaxed. Dad and Uncle Steve were fidgeting on the chairs at the front of the room. A dreamy melody was floating around the room from a harp, played by another of Eve's friends. People were chatting quietly. Nat and I went to wait for Eve at the back. Then, Siena hurried in from the entrance hall, whispering to us that Eve had arrived. We were ushered outside to meet her. She looked beautiful. Her long black hair had been set in soft curls falling gently round her face. The cloak and tiara made her look like the Snow Queen. She grinned and headed straight for us, arms outstretched.

'Mind the dresses!' I said.

'You look gorgeous!' we all said together.

Nat said, 'Jinx!' and we all giggled.

We were interrupted by the photographer who took lots of pictures in front of the tree. After several photos, it was time to go into the ceremony. Siena popped her head round the door, to let them know, and gave us the thumbs up. Eve squeezed our hands and we made our entrance.

The room had been darkened so that the lights of the candles and lanterns flickered romantically. The harpist played as we walked slowly to the front of the room. Dad's mouth hung open, and when we reached the front, I could see tears in his eyes. Eve and Dad held hands and beamed at each other. Then the celebrant began her speech. We sang Eve's favourite carol, 'In the Bleak Mid-Winter,' at the beginning, and Dad's favourite carol, 'O Come All Ye Faithful,' at the end. Before we knew it, the celebrant was saying, 'I now pronounce you man and wife. You may kiss the bride.' But Dad was already kissing the bride! Embarrassing!

Afterwards, there were lots more photos and then the meal. It was like a big Christmas dinner, with party poppers and party hats and everyone telling the jokes from the crackers. The speeches made the adults laugh a lot and go all gooey.

'When does the disco start?' Nat whispered to me while Eve was making a speech.

'Not for ages,' I whispered back. I glanced over at Zoe, who was yawning behind her napkin.

The disco was the best bit. Zoe and I danced to nearly every song. 'Well you've really done it now!' she shouted in my ear as we danced.

'Done what?' I shouted back.

'Gone and got yourself a wicked stepmother!'

I gave her a playful shove. She shoved me back. I fell over. She tripped over me and we ended up in a laughing heap on the dance floor.

By the end of the evening we were exhausted. At eleven o'clock Dad told us we needed to get ready to go home. Uncle Steve was going to take us. Dad and Eve were staying at the Manor for the night. Nat and

I went up to a bedroom where we could get changed. As we took off our bridesmaid's dresses, it was like stripping the magic away. Suddenly I felt normal again as we stood there, in our jeans, looking in the full-length mirror.

'I don't want to go home,' said Nat's reflection.

'Me neither,' mine agreed.

'Don't go on about it to Mum,' I said.

'I won't.'

'It's weird, isn't it?'

'Yeah.'

Uncle Steve knocked on the door. 'Ready?'

'Coming,' I shouted.

We went to kiss Dad and Eve goodbye. Eve had changed out of her wedding dress earlier in the evening. She was wearing a long black evening dress, which made her look very elegant.

'I've got something for you.' She handed us each a small box, wrapped in silver paper, with a ribbon tied around it. 'You can open them now,' she said, seeing our hesitation. 'I didn't want to give them to you during the speeches. I wanted it to be more personal.' Inside each was a silver locket, with intricate Celtic knotwork on the front. My name was inscribed on the back of mine, and Nat's on hers.

'They're beautiful. Thank you,' I said.

'Thank you,' Nat echoed.

Eve beamed.

'Hope all goes well at home,' Dad said. 'Bye, sweethearts.' They kissed us and waved us off as we left in Uncle Steve's car.

When Mum opened the door, she was smiling. Well, her mouth was smiling. She talked briefly with Uncle Steve, then we said goodbye to him and went inside.

'How did it go then?' she asked.

Nat and I glanced at each other. 'Fine,' I said.

'Did you have a good time?'

'Yes,' Nat replied.

'I bet you two were beautiful.'

'We looked like princesses, Mum,' Nat offered, a bit too enthusiastically. I gave her a look.

'Well, that's good then,' sighed Mum. 'Time for bed, I think. You must be tired.'

It was midnight.

Saturday 22nd December

So here I am, still in bed and it's eleven o'clock! It's the beginning of the Christmas holidays. This morning, Dad and Eve are off to Scotland on their honeymoon. Won't see my dad 'til next year, as they're not back until the 2nd January. They might see some snow in the hills. I'm sure we won't get any here. And New Year's Eve in Scotland is meant to be brilliant. What do they call it? (Had to look up the spelling) Hogmanay! I can just imagine Dad prancing around in a kilt! LOL Och aye the noo!

I messaged Zoe.

> Me: Hey BFF! Did U enjoy yesterday?

No reply. Still asleep I suspect!
About an hour later:

> Zoe: Hey BFF! Just got up! Yeah. CWL! Fancy going Christmas shopping? Got to get pressies for Mum and Rick
> Me: K Got stuff 2 get 4 everyone! Haven't done any yet with wedding fever going on til now

So, we've been shopping all day. Got some great presents for Mum, Nat, Dad and Eve. I hope they like them. Won't be able to give Dad's and Eve's 'til after

New Year. Won't really feel the same.

Mum actually went to a Christmas party last night, with people from work. She hadn't told us about that, before now. I'm glad she went out. I asked her if she'd had a good time and she said yes. She told me she'd got talking to this woman she didn't know very well, but she'd made her feel much more positive about the coming year, as she had also been through a divorce. It felt nice that Mum told me this. I felt like she was treating me like a friend, not just a little kid.

Feeling really happy today.

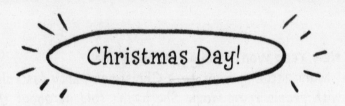

Christmas Day!

You don't need me to tell you the date today, Dear Diary!

The usual suspects came round to have Christmas dinner with us. Grandma has come to stay for a couple of days. Auntie Sadie and Uncle Eddie (Mum's brother) came down with our cousins, Dan and Tom. Dinner was yummy: Turkey, pigs in blankets, cranberry sauce... okay, Brussels sprouts too, but I didn't eat the disgusting things! Dad always tells the joke - 'What's the difference between Brussels sprouts and bogeys?' And we all shout, 'You can't get your children to eat Brussels sprouts!' And Dad makes this kind of bu-bum sound, and raps the table like a drum. We still laugh at his awful jokes, even though we've heard them a million times. It felt like there was an empty space at the table today, even though all the chairs were filled. This is the first Christmas Day without Dad. So much has happened since that day, nearly a year ago, when Dad blurted out, 'I'm leaving.'

He phoned just after lunch. It was so good to hear his voice. He's having a brilliant time and said they've had lots of snow and the food is great. He just finished his Christmas dinner. We had it on speakerphone and Nat asked him to tell the Brussels sprout joke! We laughed. Mum was watching us, and even she smiled. We didn't speak to Eve. Dad said she was asleep, but that she sent her love.

Uncle Eddie organised the silly party games, as usual, after lunch. He thinks it's hilarious to pass a bin liner round the circle, filled with old clothes and stuff from charity shops: a big floppy hat, sunglasses with palm trees growing out of them, a big flowery blouse, false beard, wellies, a bra with massive cups, etc. When the music stops, you have to take an item out and put it on, until the bag is empty. Then, everyone does the conga around the house, looking ridiculous. The adults laugh so much they have to sit down for half an hour, exhausted. Usually they watch the Queen at that point. I took lots of pics on my phone to put on Instagram. I thought I'd message some to Dad, but then I decided not to. It might make him sad.

We also had to play pass the parcel, charades and Who's Who. As soon as we could, Nat, Tom, Dan and I sneaked off upstairs to watch one of our new DVDs. The adults snoozed and boozed.

It's been a good Christmas. I'm writing this at 11p.m. I've enjoyed today, but Nat just came into my room and said, 'I wish Dad was here.' I gave her a hug. I do too.

Sunday 30th December

Dad sent us a postcard. Somehow it managed to get to us, despite Christmas holidays and post. Nat picked it up and came running to show me. She read it out.

'Dear Nat and Lou,
Having a lovely, chilly time in Scotland. The mountains are beautiful in the snow. Been skiing today. Didn't break a leg. Phew! Can't wait to see you NEXT YEAR!
All my love, Dad.'

No mention of Eve. 'Can I see it please?' I took the card from Nat and read it myself. I turned it over to look at the white peaks against a brilliant blue sky.
I read it again.
'Can I put it in my room, Lou?' Nat asked.
I smiled at her. 'Yeah, go on then.'
She can't wait 'til Dad comes back.

New Year's Day

Dear Diary,

Just waking up (11.47am).

Well, that was the most boring New Year's Eve for a thirteen-year-old. I wanted to have a party, but Mum said we'd just have a quiet family New Year. So, it was just the three of us. We played some board games and ate pizza. She let us stay up to watch the New Year celebrations in London, on TV. I'd love to be there and watch the actual fireworks. As soon as that was over, she said it was time for bed.

Zoe messaged me earlier.

Zoe: Happy New Year BFF! 😃😃😃
Me: Happy New Year! ☹
Zoe: ZUP?
Me: Bored. What U up 2?
Zoe: Party. Mum, Rick and all the adults are drunk. Mum has been doing animal impressions and trying to do charades ROFL U shud've been here
Me: Wish I was!
Zoe: AW. Night night BFF. And happy New Year!!!!! 😃😃😃

Saturday 5th January

We came to Dad and Eve's on Thursday. (They got back on Tuesday.) Nat was pinging around like popcorn, by the time Dad arrived for us. He was so pleased to see us; he threw his arms around us and held us tight for far too long. Nat gave him the most massive bear hug. Well, so did I. Mum was subdued. She didn't ask about the honeymoon. (Why would she?) I didn't feel guilty leaving her for a few days though. We haven't seen Dad for two weeks.

It was like Christmas Day all over again at Dad's. Eve hugged us and said she bet we'd had a good Christmas with Mum. That was nice of her. They still had a tree up. There was a whole new set of presents to open. (Lots of Scottish ones!) They'd bought me some more Celtic jewellery to go with my bridesmaid necklace. Silver earrings and a bracelet. We also got a really cute cuddly Scottie dog, each. Nat cuddled hers all day!

We had a buffet tea. No turkey, thankfully. (Had enough of that over the last few weeks, with turkey risotto, turkey pasta, turkey, blah blah blah.) After tea, we played a new board game that Dad had bought us. Then Eve lit lots of candles and we crashed out and watched good old Mary Poppins again. Nat fell asleep. Both of us were cuddled up to Dad. It's been a cosy, lazy day.

We had to come home tonight because Eve said we probably needed to get ready for school on Monday. Dad (and Mum) agreed. Boooo!

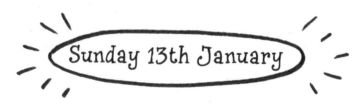

Sunday 13th January

One year today - Dad left.

Just been reading about it again. I'm so glad I've got you, Dear Diary. Things feel so different now. But not in such a bad way. This time last year, I thought my whole world had broken, never to be fixed again. It seems to have patched up okay though.

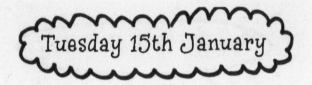

Tuesday 15th January

Dear Diary,

A very strange thing happened today.
Mum was sitting at the breakfast table this morning, with a letter in her hand. She had a serious look on her face as she stared hard at it.

'What's up, Mum?' I asked, coming into the kitchen.

She looked up, as if I'd startled her. 'What? Oh, hi love. Er, nothing's up. Would you like some toast?' She slid the letter half under the other post and got up.

'Yes please,' I answered, looking at the corner of the letter peeping out. 'Are you sure there's nothing up? You looked worried.'

She tried to act all casual and said, 'Oh, did I? Just concentrating. Something I didn't quite understand.'

As I was about to leave, I caught her again staring at the letter.

'Mum,' I said, 'Please tell me what's wrong.'

'There's nothing wrong, love. It's fine. You'd better get going. You'll miss the bus.' She held the letter behind her back. Did she think I was seven years old?

'There is something wrong. It's that letter. I'm not stupid, Mum. It's something bad, isn't it?'

She looked at me for a while, biting her lip. Then she looked at the letter. 'It's nothing, really. Go to school. Go on.'

What else could I do? I ran for my bus. But, I've been

198

thinking about it all day. Zoe said not to worry about it; that adults always had stuff they were worrying about. Probably nothing serious. But, it wasn't a bill or anything. I'd seen lots of words. My mind started to think of all sorts of scenarios of bad news that people could be breaking. Did Grandma have cancer? Was Mum losing her job? Was Uncle Eddie dying?

I had to know.

When I got home I quizzed her about it again. She tried to put me off, but I wasn't letting go. I've got better at being more pushy - persistent - this last year.

Eventually, she gave in. 'Oh well, you'll find out sooner or later. I just didn't know how you'd take it.'

I prepared myself for something terrible.

Mum said, 'You see, I don't understand it at all. You seemed to be getting on so well with her.'

'What? Who?' I asked.

'You'd better read it for yourself, then you'll really believe it. I can't take it in, but maybe you can make sense of it.' She handed me the type-written letter. I've written it all out here:

Linda,

I want you to know something, which must be kept between ourselves. It will be for your benefit as well as mine, I'm sure you'll agree. Up until now I have been very nice to your daughters. In fact, we have been getting along very well indeed, at least as far as they're aware. They really like me and we've bonded so well you wouldn't believe it. However, I never wanted your children and now I've got Mike to finally marry me, I want them out of my life as much as possible. So, I want you to make excuses to Mike as to why they can't come here. He can obviously come to you and take them out, but I don't want them here much anymore. I've got my own agenda for family with Mike. I realise in the long term we will need to rethink the strategy, but for now this will have to do. This is win-win if you'll help me. You get your girls mainly to yourself. No more lonely weekends. No more being jealous of their new stepmother!

If you won't help me in this, remember, your girls really like me and I could get them to like me a LOT more, believe me! I'm sure you don't want to lose out to their stepmother, do you? If you tell Mike any of this, I will make your life a misery. Believe me, I can!

I hope you will see the benefits of co-operating.

Eve

My eyes filled with tears as I read it. It hit me like a punch in the head. I had to read it several times to take it in. Even then I was speechless.

Mum looked anxiously at me. 'I don't know what to say. She had me fooled too, love. I thought she genuinely liked you and Nat. I don't know what to do.'

'We've got to tell Dad,' I said, immediately. 'He'll have it out with her. She was just stringing us along. How could she be so convincing? That's evil! The witch! The lying, scheming, two-faced, evil witch!' I could feel tears running down my cheeks now. Mum hugged me.

'Do you think we should tell Nat?' she asked, as if I would know what to do.

'I don't...'

'Tell me what?' said Nat, coming into the room. 'What's the matter? Why is Lou crying?'

Mum and I looked at each other, not knowing what to do. I was so angry that I blurted out, 'It's Eve. She's been lying to us all along. She doesn't really like us. She hates us, in fact. She doesn't want us to go to Dad's anymore.'

'Not go to Dad's?' Nat burst into tears. 'But I want to see Dad!' she wailed. 'I want to see Dad!'

It took a while for Mum to calm us down. Nat was so upset and I was so angry. Mum told us she had to play it carefully. I insisted we should tell him, but she said not yet. She needed to think. She would handle it for a while and did we think we could play along with Eve's demands for now? We nodded, dazed and confused. Mum seemed to be hatching her own plan.

Dad phoned later this evening, to arrange to pick us up on Saturday, and I heard Mum begin her story.

'Well you see, Mike, Nat has been feeling really unsure about things since the wedding and Christmas. I think it would do her good if you could visit them here, or take them somewhere neutral for a while... No, I don't think they should... No, I think it should just be you. I'm sure she'll get over it. She just needs some security for a while...Thanks...Yeah! I appreciate you being so understanding.'

'Was that Dad, Mum?' I asked, coming into the room.

She hadn't realised I was listening from the hall, and looked a little startled. 'Yes love, everything's sorted; for a few weeks, at least. You must make sure you and Nat don't say anything about Eve. I know it'll be hard for you Lou. I know how angry you are and how much she's hurt you. I'm sure your chance to say what you think of her will come.'

I nodded.

I'm still reeling from the shock. How could she do this? What a liar, and after she told me last summer to trust her! She must have been planning to do this all along, after they got married. I thought of some strong words I wanted to say to her face! I won't insult you, Dear Diary, by writing them here, because they are not pleasant! Earlier, I pulled off the necklace she gave me at the wedding. I yanked the chain with such force that, as it snapped, the locket flew across the room.

I stamped on it and growled, 'I don't want your

bribery. I don't want anything you've ever given me.'

I deleted all the photographs of the mural, we'd painted together, from my phone and Instagram feed.

'Sucking up to us to get our dad. You witch!' I shouted across the bedroom.

Nat came in and I wish I'd kept quiet, she kept asking me why Eve didn't like us anymore. She was worried that she'd done something wrong.

'Do you think I wasn't a very good bridesmaid?' she asked, looking at my broken locket on the floor and touching hers, around her neck.

'Of course you were, Nat. You were perfect. It's all to do with grown-up things, complicated stuff.'

She went back to her room, shaking her head and mumbling to herself.

What I don't understand is why we can't just tell Dad. There again, it will break his heart and he might get divorced again. But, maybe he should. He can't stay with *her* now. But, I have to trust Mum on this one. She seemed to have a plan.

I messaged Zoe:

Me: Turns out U were right about Eve. She IS evil!
Zoe: Zouch! ZUP?
Me: Tell you tomorrow. Too much to type
Zoe: Facetime?
Me: Nah. Need to sleep. Tell U tomoz
Zoe: Here 4 ya. Xoxo
Me: xoxo

Wednesday 16th January

At school, today, I told Zoe everything. At first, she thought it was the juiciest bit of gossip ever.

'It's like a Coronation Street plot, isn't it?' she enthused. 'She really has turned out to be the wicked stepmother after all, hasn't she? Good job your Mum's got a plan, or who knows what she would've done with you!'

'It's not funny!' I snapped. 'This is my life we're talking about, not some stupid soap or, even stupider still, some fairy-tale. Anyway, they have happy endings. I can't see how this will.'

She said sorry.

'We're seeing Dad on Saturday. I don't know what we'll say to him. He thinks Eve's wonderful. Little does he know!'

'Maybe you should tell him, even if your Mum doesn't want you to.'

'No, I've promised I won't, and so has Nat. We'll see what Mum's planning first.'

'Okay, but if I was you, I'd have to go round there and tell her what I thought of her.'

'Yeah, we tried that once and we just ended up looking stupid.'

Zoe shrugged. 'That was different. We made a mistake. You've got the letter as evidence this time.'

I don't know what to do. Just when everything was going well.

Dad came to pick us up. We were both really nervous that we might let something out. He took us to an interactive arts and crafts exhibition. It was okay. There was loads to do and it distracted us for a while. I made jewellery and did some batik. Nat also made jewellery and did some glass painting. I noticed Dad being particularly lovely to Nat, probably because of Mum's excuse on the phone. But, in between the crafty bits, he kept talking about Eve. How she wished she could have come and she hoped we were okay. Nat and I kept giving each other knowing looks, wanting desperately to blurt it all out, about the letter and how Evil Eve was a two-faced schemer. But somehow, we managed to make it to the end of the day without saying anything. The atmosphere was strained and Dad felt it.

As we drove home in the car he said, 'I'm sorry it's been such an odd day. It won't be long before you feel okay about coming home with me again, will it? But you just take all the time you need, love.' He looked in the mirror at Nat.

She smiled weakly at him and turned in panic to me. But I couldn't help, because I knew if I opened my big mouth, it would all come out. I felt like a pan, simmering with the lid on and starting to bubble over.

Been out with Dad again today. This deception has been going on for two weeks now and it's doing my head in. Each time it's getting harder and harder, and Dad is more and more desperate for things to get back to how they were before the wedding. He keeps asking Mum if she thinks Nat is ready to come back yet, or even if I could come on my own. But Mum keeps putting him off with more excuses. I don't want to see Evil Eve ever again! I feel a complete fool for being taken in by her. I do feel sorry for Dad though. I tried to talk to Mum about it when we got back.

'We've got to tell him the truth, Mum. This can't go on forever. He shouldn't be with her when she's such a liar. I mean, what does she really want from Dad? Maybe she's plotting to bump him off and get all his money.'

Mum laughed! Actually laughed like a hyena! 'Lou! Don't be so melodramatic! Anyway, your dad hasn't got any money.'

'Well, we should still tell him about her. He should get a divorce. Show him the letter.'

'No Lou. It's tricky. It's a delicate situation. He won't believe me and then who knows what he'll do.'

'But you've got the evidence, Mum,' I insisted.

Mum wouldn't discuss it any further and started to get cross with me. I was getting more and more frustrated with her, so, I came upstairs and messaged Zoe.

Me: U there?
Zoe: Yep
Me: It's horrible
Zoe: ?
Me: Dad situation! Feel like he's being lied to by everyone! Hasn't a clue what's really going on
Zoe: U got to remember who started this in the first place last January
Me: Him. Yeah. But still, we've moved on
Zoe: This is what happens with adults. They're idiots
Me: Mum seems to be taking it okay. Actually think she's glad we're not seeing Eve
Zoe: Course she is. I've told you B4 what I'd do. U should have it out with yr dad
Me: Yeah

I've thought all evening about what Zoe has been saying for the past two weeks. I can't keep this up for much longer. Anyway, it couldn't go on forever. I've decided to confront Mum about it this week and tell her that I'm going to tell Dad if she doesn't.

Thursday 7th February

Dear Diary,

I'm at Dad's. Long story. Things couldn't get much worse now. My life is horrible! Horrible! Horrible!
This is what happened today.
In the afternoon, I was thinking I need to pluck up the courage to talk to Mum tonight. In geography, I was plotting in my head, how the conversation would go, when the Deputy Head came into the classroom and asked to speak to me. I followed her down the corridor, to her room. What was going on? I knew I'd been a bit distracted all week, so maybe I was in trouble. She made me sit down.
'Now Louise,' she said, 'I don't want you to get too worried about what I'm going to tell you, because it'll be fine.'

Panic!

'Your Mum's been in a car accident but...'

A car accident!' I yelled, jumping to my feet.

Mrs. Evans gently put her hands on my shoulders and made me sit down again. She sat beside me.
'Yes. But she's going to be okay. She has some injuries to her leg and ribs, but nothing life threatening, so she

will be alright.'

My mind was racing. I could feel tears running down my cheeks. Mrs. Evans gave me some tissues and put her arm round my shoulders.

'Your Dad has gone to fetch your sister. Then he's coming to get you and take you to the hospital. I shouldn't think he'll be long, so you just wait here. I'm going to get you a glass of water.'

She left the room. The tears kept coming and, in my head, I just kept shouting out for Mum. Mrs. Evans came back with the water. I sipped it and wiped my eyes. She talked to me the whole time; reassuring me.

Dad arrived after about ten minutes, but it felt more like ten hours. 'Lou. Are you alright? Come on, love, let's get to the hospital, then you'll be able to see your Mum. She's going to be okay.' He bundled me out of the door, saying thanks to Mrs. Evans as he went.

Nat was in the car. She'd been crying. She clung to me as I got in and I found that I was now the one saying, 'It's going to be alright.' Dad was trying to be reassuring as he drove, but I could tell he was anxious.

'I've spoken to them at the hospital and she is going straight to theatre for an operation on her leg. So, we won't be able to see her straight away, but the doctors will be able to tell us what's going on.'

When we arrived at the hospital, a very nice doctor explained that Mum had no critical injuries and that she would be 100% back to normal when she recovered. She has broken her leg and cracked some ribs and has a few cuts and bruises. Apparently, she pulled out of a parking space at the side of the road, without looking, and a car had gone into her. Mum's car was a write-off but, thankfully, she wasn't.

We sat around, for what seemed like an endless time, in the waiting area. We drank lots of vending machine drinks and ate junk food. Finally, we were allowed to see Mum. By this time, it was mid-evening. She was sleeping on the ward. She looked a bit bruised, but much better than I'd expected her to. We were allowed to give her a gentle kiss.

'We'll come back tomorrow,' whispered Dad, 'so you can speak to her. We'd better go back to your place and get some things, and then we'll go back to mine. I phoned Eve before I picked you up. She said she'd get your beds ready. She'll be relieved to hear everything's going to be okay.'

It hadn't dawned on us until then, that we would have to stay at Dad's while Mum was in hospital.

'But, we can't stay at yours!' I blurted out. 'Not after... Mum wouldn't... Eve...'

Dad looked confused. And who could blame him, when he had no idea what I was trying not to tell him!

He said, 'It'll be okay. I know things have been difficult lately, especially for you Nat, but maybe it will help you to feel at home with us again. You'll remember all the things you liked about staying over at our house.'

Nat begged, 'I don't want to. Please Dad. You come and stay at home till Mum gets back, please.'

'It'll be okay love, I promise,' he said, scooping her up and giving her a kiss. 'Come on, it's been a traumatic day for you both. Let's go and leave Mum in peace 'til tomorrow.'

We went back home and picked up some things for the next few days. I had a key, so we were able to get in. While we were in our bedrooms, I whispered to Nat to just go straight to bed when we got there. We just wouldn't speak to Eve. I also messaged Zoe about what's happened.

Me: Mum's been in a car crash!
Zoe: Zoo-zinder-eenies! Is she okay?
Me: Yes. Saw her earlier but was sleeping. She's had op. Will be K. Going 2 see her tomoz properly
Zoe: Say hi from me. Where R U?
Me: Dad's
Zoe: Yikes! 😵
Me: IKR
Zoe: What u going to do about Evil Eve?
Me: keep out of her way
Zoe: U shud say something
Me: I can't
Zoe: See what she's like with u
Me: Yeah 😐

When we arrived at Dad's, Eve greeted us with arms open ready to hug us. She was full of false, comforting, sympathetic words that meant nothing. I turned away as she tried to hug me, and Nat hid behind me. Eve said we must be shattered and what a terrible ordeal we'd had, then she went to make us a drink. I told Dad that we just wanted to go to bed. So, we went upstairs and he brought us up a hot chocolate. Nat has been asleep for ages, and I'm going to try and sleep now. I'm sooooo tired!

Friday 8th February

I woke early, anxious to see Mum. It was 6:30 and no one else was awake. I sneaked downstairs and put the light on to write to you, Dear Diary, because I didn't want to wake Nat. I was thinking about how I'd been planning to have an argument with Mum about needing to tell Dad about the letter. Imagine if she'd died yesterday! I really want to speak to her today. And now we're staying at Eve's and she's pretending to be all kind and sympathetic, but I saw the frown she gave Dad when she thought we weren't looking. She definitely doesn't want us here.

Someone's coming!

Sorry for the abrupt finish, Diary. Eve came down. I'd almost finished writing to you, when, from behind me, Eve's voice said, 'Hi Lou. How are you this morning?' I didn't even look up. I slammed you shut. 'Fine!' I stormed past her, upstairs back to my room and lay on the bottom bunk, in the dark, for a while. I could hear Nat breathing heavily above me. Maybe this was the time to tell Eve what I thought of her. Get it out in the open. But then we'd have to live here for who knew how many days, having blurted all that out. I couldn't do it. I felt paralysed. Then Zoe's voice started seeping through the darkness.

'You should tell her what you think of her!'

'I can't!' said my voice in my head.

'You should tell her!' insisted Zoe.

'I can't! I hissed.

'Tell her!' Zoe screeched at me.

I couldn't stand it. I got out of bed and walked determinedly to the kitchen, where I could hear Eve moving around. The radio was on and she was singing. My stomach was churning. She had her back to me as I came to the door.

I summoned all my courage. 'I really don't get you,' I said, standing in the doorway with my arms folded.

She turned round. 'Sorry?' Then she turned pale, as she saw my face.

'You should be!' I said. 'You should be sorry, but you're not. You're acting like you've done nothing wrong, but you don't fool me. I know the truth.' I was trying hard to handle it like I thought Zoe would.

'If I have done something wrong, I need to know what it is, so I can put it right.' she said, coming towards me. 'Come and sit down, Louise, and we can talk.'

How could she act so innocently? I refused to sit down.

'You wrote my Mum that scheming letter and you say you don't know what you've done?' I was beginning to raise my voice.

'What letter?' she asked.

I wanted to punch her! 'You know very well what letter. Why don't you stop pretending?'

'Lou, I really don't know what you're talking about. What was in the letter?'

'You know what! How you never liked me and Nat. You just used us to get Dad. Now you don't want to see us and you don't want Dad to know what a two-faced cow you are!' I shouted the last bit at her, though I couldn't quite bring myself to call her what Zoe had suggested.

At this point, Dad came down the stairs, in his PJs, looking bleary-eyed. 'What's going on?'

Now I was scared and it suddenly dawned on me what I'd done. However, I was in too deep to stop. 'Ask her about the letter she wrote Mum.'

'What letter?' Dad said.

'I don't know what she means,' said Eve. 'She says I wrote a nasty letter to Linda, saying I didn't want to see the girls; that I'd just been using them to get you or something like that.'

Dad looked confused. He rubbed his hands over his face and through his hair. He pushed past me and went to sit down at the kitchen table.

'What's this all about, Lou? Is this something to do with why you haven't been coming here over the last few weeks?'

'Yes,' I said, 'Mum said we should keep quiet about it and she would sort it out. Eve was blackmailing Mum!'

'Mike, you must believe I'd never do such a thing. It's ridiculous. I've really missed the girls!'

Nat came down at this point. She just stood listening to what was going on.

'I do believe you,' Dad said to Eve. 'This is crazy. But there must be some explanation.'

'The explanation is, she fooled us all, Dad. She's been stringing us along from the start.'

Eve protested. 'Lou, I did not write a letter to your Mum and I do care for you and Nat. I am telling the truth.' Her eyes pleaded with mine. For a fleeting moment, I wanted to believe her.

As if reading my mind, she said, 'You've got to believe me. There's no way on earth I would do such a horrible thing! Someone else must have written it. Someone who's got it in for me, but I've no idea who.'

'I think she's telling the truth,' Nat suddenly piped up. We all looked at her. She was standing in the hallway, with her hands on her hips, looking very serious.

Eve said, 'I am, Nat, I am. Thank you for believing me. Lou, please, listen. I am telling the truth.'

'Why do you believe her, Nat? She's just pretending again because Dad's here,' I said.

But Nat shook her head. 'I don't think she is. She's always been nice to us. It doesn't make sense.'

There was a long, long pause. They all stared at me. I was wavering. 'Well if you didn't write it then... who did?'

Eve's eyes began to fill up. 'I won't rest until it's proved that I didn't do this. I couldn't hurt you like that.'

Dad said, 'We will get to the bottom of this.'

I wasn't sure if he was angry with me, or just angry, full-stop. Then he softened. 'But now, we should get dressed and go and see your mum.'

As I turned to go upstairs, I glanced back at Eve. She had turned away from me and was making toast. I was still suspicious.

On the way to the hospital no one said much. I messaged Zoe to tell her I'd tackled Eve. This is what she said:

Zoe: Awesome! Proud of you!
Me: I was petrified
Zoe: So, do you believe her?
Me: Dunno what to believe
Zoe: 😑

The only truth is, that I don't have a clue if Eve is telling the truth or not!

When we got to the hospital, I tried to put all that out of my mind. We put on our cheeriest faces and went onto the ward. Mum was sitting up in bed and when she saw us she beamed. We ran up to the bed and almost fell on top of her, trying to hug her.

'Careful,' Dad said. Then we both started speaking at once, trying to tell her how relieved we were that she was okay. She just smiled and and said, 'Oooh, that hurts.' And 'Don't make me laugh!' She told us a bit about the accident and how she felt really stupid, but grateful to be alive. Her first words when she came round, after the operation, had been about us and where we were staying. She said to Dad that she hoped it wasn't too much trouble. She was sorry to have caused such worry. She babbled on for ages. It was a huge relief all round to see her so perky, if battered and bruised. Nat asked when she'd be coming home.

Mum told us that she'd have to stay in for at least a week. 'So I guess you'll have to stay with Dad, I'm sorry.' She bit her lip and didn't look at him.

'It's no trouble at all,' Dad reassured her. 'You just get lots of rest.'

Mum looked anxious.

'So, with that in mind, we should leave now. We'll come back tomorrow.'

We kissed Mum goodbye. My head is spinning, but I'm sooooo relieved that she's okay.

Dear Diary,

We went to visit Mum on Saturday, yesterday and tonight. Her cheeks were rosier by tonight and she seemed a little less tired each day. Dad insisted that we shouldn't miss too much school, so we're visiting in the evenings. Everyone at school wanted to hear all the details of what had happened to Mum. I was the most popular girl to talk to today.

Zoe is intrigued by the letter mystery. She wants to play detective and solve it, of course.

'Do you really think Eve is innocent?'

'I dunno. Being with her again has made me realise I like her. It's hard to believe it's all an act, she's too... genuine,' I mused. 'We've gone round and round in circles, trying to work out who could've written it.'

'Well, it has to be someone who has it in for her. Or maybe someone's got it in for your Mum.'

'But how would this hurt Mum? It doesn't make her look bad, only Eve.'

'Yes, but it has made your mum lie to your dad. And maybe they knew that sooner or later it would all have to come out. No, maybe it's your dad they want to get!'

She was totally absorbed in it now. 'Whoa! Slow down Miss Marple! It's too confusing!' Just then the buzzer sounded for next lesson, so we went our separate ways. I could think of nothing else throughout the whole of the afternoon.

Back at Dad's, there was still some tension between us and Eve. Then, out of the blue, Eve announced that she would like to go and see Mum. We all looked at her in shock.

Dad said, 'I'm not sure that would be a good idea.'

'I really need to talk to her about this letter,' Eve insisted. 'I don't want her to think badly of me. I'd like her to know I'm concerned about her too. And, we could kick around some ideas about who might have written the letter.'

Dad said, 'I don't think it's the right time.'

'What do you think, girls?' asked Eve.

We shook our heads.

Eve said we couldn't just leave the issue hanging for much longer. It's true, it is driving us all crazy. She said she was going to go to the hospital tomorrow. Dad made some more protests, but there was no dissuading her. Nat and I came to bed, in case an argument started. I haven't heard any shouting yet...

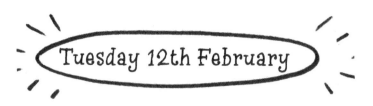

Tuesday 12th February

This is a long one, Dear Diary. But I know you want the whole story.

Today, my stomach has been twisting like a tornado. I knew what time Eve was going to see Mum. It was during science, just after double maths. I hate maths at the best of times, but this morning I had to leave the room because I thought I was going to be sick. As I stood in the toilets, I had a thought. Maybe if I caught a bus straight away, I could go down to the hospital and try to smooth things between Mum and Eve. I'd never bunked off school in my life, so I felt even sicker. I went back to my lesson and asked the teacher if I could go to the medical room. As I really did look white, and about to throw up, he didn't have any objection. I headed furtively (good word) out of the side door and within five minutes I was on a bus to the hospital. It was so easy.

The bus seemed to take ages. Loads of people wanted to get on and off at every stop. I felt like a fugitive (even better word)! I zipped up my coat, trying to hide my school uniform. I was taking deep breaths to try and fend off the nausea that kept rising from my stomach. A woman asked me if I was okay.

I told her I was feeling sick.

She was really kind. 'Here you are, dear, have a mint. I always suck one if I'm feeling a bit travel sick. It's these buses, they lurch about all over the place.'

I took the mint and thanked her. It did help. I was glad to get off the bus and gulp some fresh air. It was only a few minutes' walk to the hospital, but I realised Eve would have been there for some time now. Or maybe she'd chickened out and hadn't come? I'd have to go in and find out. I'd only just got inside the main entrance when I saw her hurrying towards me. She had her head down and didn't see me at first.

'Eve!' I called.

She looked up. Her face was pale, but as she recognised me it flushed bright red.

'Lou! What are you doing here? Why aren't you at school?'

'I couldn't bear it. I had to come and see what was going on between you and Mum. I thought I might be able to help. Have you seen her?'

'Yes. Yes, we've talked. Look, we should phone your Dad and get him to take you back to school. You'll get into real trouble if we don't sort it out.'

'No. I want to know what happened with you and Mum. Did you get to the bottom of it? Is she upset? Should I go and see her?'

Eve looked flustered. 'I don't think you should go in there right now. She needs some time on her own.'

I felt anger rising. 'Why? What have you said to her? Have you upset her? You better not have. Dad was right, you shouldn't have come.'

She went to put her arm round me. I shrugged away. She said, 'Come on. I'm going to call your Dad.'

I said, 'No, please don't. He'll kill me. I'll go back to school. They think I'm in the medical room. No one will have even missed me. It's organised chaos there. You still haven't told me about the letter.'

'I can't, Lou.' She hesitated, fiddling with her handbag. 'You need to talk about it together, with your Mum and Dad here. You're coming back this evening, aren't you?'

'Yes, but why can't you tell me? Something awful's happened. I know it. Just tell me!'

Eve was nearly in tears. 'You shouldn't have come, Lou. I'm taking you back to school. I won't tell your Dad you were here, but you've got to wait 'til later for explanations.'

We got on the bus together and sat in silence all the way back to school. It was lunchtime when we got there.

'Are you sure you'll be okay? I'll come and make excuses for you if you like?' she offered.

'I'll be fine!' I snapped and stormed back into school.

When Dad picked me up from school, I looked at Nat in the back of the car. She was white as a sheet and I felt terrified. Dad made reassuring noises all the way to the hospital, but at the same time he looked anxious.

*

As we walked onto the ward we put on our best plastic smiles. Mum wasn't looking for us eagerly, like she normally did. We came around the bottom of her bed, putting on the chirpiest voices we could muster, to say hi. I was about to kiss her, but she looked at me like a frightened rabbit. Then she looked down at the bed clothes and burst into tears. Dad quickly drew the curtains round the bed.

'What's wrong, Mum? What is it? Did Eve upset you?' I blurted out.

Nat flung her arms round Mum's neck. Mum continued to sob. She put her hand over her mouth, trying to stifle the noise. It was very loud. A nurse popped her head in, and asked if Mum needed her. Mum shook her head and Dad said we just needed some time alone. Dad gave her the tissue box and we waited for her to stop crying.

'I'm so sorry,' she sobbed. 'You'll all hate me.'

We looked puzzled. Then Nat said, 'Don't be silly Mum, we love you.' She clung tightly to Mum's neck and kissed her cheek several times.

'Yes, you will. You'll hate me,' she sniffed.

Dad said, 'I'm sorry. I should have stopped Eve from coming.'

'It's not her fault,' Mum snivelled. 'She hasn't done anything wrong. I'm sorry. I've been so mean about her. I never gave her a chance.'

Dad asked, 'Did you figure out who wrote that letter?'

I felt awful. This was all my fault. I shouldn't have blurted it out to Eve. Maybe Zoe wasn't always right.

Mum looked into each of our faces with frightened eyes. Then she focused on the curtain, straight ahead, and took a deep ragged breath. 'I wrote the letter. At least, I got a friend to type it and post it, but I told her exactly what to write.' There was a pause, as we all looked at Mum in shock. She continued. 'I wanted to make Eve look bad. I hated her getting so close to the girls. I hated her for breaking up my family. I hated her for having a fairy-tale wedding. I had to stop you all from being so... happy. Happy without me!'

She started crying again. No one could speak. She struggled to regain some composure. 'When Eve came to see me today, I was totally rude to her. I told her to get out and I was about to call a nurse and have her removed. And then she started talking about the letter. I wanted to slink under the bed clothes and hide. I tried to get her to go away, but she wouldn't, and as she talked I began to realise how much she cared about you all. She even seemed to care about me, for some strange reason. She wanted to find out who could have done such a thing. The more she spoke, the worse I felt, until I just broke down and told her the whole story. I thought she'd storm off and I'd find myself fighting a custody battle soon, but she didn't. She kept reassuring me that she didn't want to take my place and never could. We talked for a long time about things. She told me how much you love me and talk about me. I felt so foolish. But you know what? For the first time, since the divorce, I felt... relieved.'

I heard words, slow and menacing coming out of my mouth. 'How could you do it, Mum? You made us think such horrible things about Eve and it was you all the time!' My voice rose in pitch as anger overcame me. 'I thought Dad was the rotten one for leaving you and us. I never understood how he could do it. But this! You are just as bad! You lied to us; you kept us from seeing Dad. You made us believe Eve was evil!'

I got up, angrily wiping tears from my eyes and marched out of the ward. I could hear Nat saying, 'It'll be okay, Mum. You didn't mean it. Don't cry Mum.'

The last thing I heard was Mum saying, 'Go after her, Mike, please. She's right.'

Dad caught up with me in the corridor. He grabbed my arm. 'Lou! Stop!'

I tried to shake him off. 'I'm not going back in Dad. I can't face her right now. I don't know what to say.'

'It's okay, love. It's fine to be angry. I know you felt the same about me a year ago.'

'I did.'

'But you gave me a chance. You were wonderful. You've been amazing the way you've accepted Eve. Now you've got to give your mum a chance. I know we're asking a lot of you and Nat, but please try. Mum needs you.'

'She needed you, Dad, but it didn't stop you doing what you wanted.'

He winced. 'That's true. I've no right to be asking you to do something I wasn't prepared to do. I don't know what else to say.'

We sat down on the blue plastic chairs in the corridor. There was silence for a long time. The past year or so was playing out on the wall in front of me, like a film. I looked at Dad. His brow was furrowed, but there was always gentleness in his eyes.

'I'd better go back in.' He hesitated, waiting for me

to get up, but I continued to sit there, staring straight ahead. He went back without me.

I sat there for ages, thinking. I'd never really understand what had gone on between him and Mum, or the reasons why he'd chosen to leave. I thought about Mum. I tried to understand why she had deceived us in such a way. If I'd forgiven Dad, then maybe I had to do the same for Mum. But, I couldn't just turn it on right now.

I messaged Zoe:

Me: I know who wrote the letter
Zoe: Zounds! Who?
Me: Mum
Zoe: Joking!!! 😲
Me: Duh!
Zoe: Zipidi-zipzangers!
Me: IKR
Zoe: Tell me all
Me: TTYL

When we got back to Dad's, I waited until Eve was alone in the kitchen. She was washing the dishes. I walked over to the sink and took up a tea towel. We worked in awkward silence for a few minutes, while I tried to form an adequate sentence.

'Eve?'

'Yes.'

'I'm sorry.'

'Accepted,' she said.

Then she turned to me and grinned. I had a sudden urge to hug her. So, I did.

Zoe has been messaging me all evening for more info, but I didn't fancy sending loads of long messages. I'd better Facetime her.

Saturday 16th February

We found out today that Mum is going to be able to come home next week. She'll have to take it easy and we're going to have to be super-helpful. I'm not sure I want to go back to hers now. I'm still angry with her. But Dad and Eve insisted that she'll need us. Eve helped us draw up a list of jobs we could do. Eve has been to see Mum a couple of times since her first visit. She and Mum seemed to be finding it helpful. I haven't been back since Tuesday, despite Dad and Nat constantly asking me to.

That evening, while we were eating supper, Eve suggested that we throw a welcome home party for Mum.

Nat cheered.

I shrugged.

Dad agreed that it would make Mum feel loved, which was what she needed. So, we started planning it. We'd make a banner on a long piece of material that Eve, Nat and I would paint. Eve would make some of her gorgeous cakes. We'd invite some of Mum's friends. Despite myself, I was getting into all the planning. It was a bit short notice, but the more people we could get, the better. So, we texted and phoned and emailed as many of Mum's friends as we could. I also messaged Zoe.

Zoe: U feeling K about your mum then?

Me: Dunno. Don't want to spoil it for Nat though
Zoe: It'll be fun
Me: 😃

I just don't know how I'll feel when I see Mum again.

Tuesday 19th February

Dear Diary,

It's half term. And today is the day Mum came home. I had butterflies.

She was discharged from the hospital at 5p.m. Eve went round to the house yesterday and got almost everything set up and ready. Today, she just had to do one or two things, like putting up the banner. Dad and Nat went to pick up Mum. I stayed with Eve. My excuse was that I was helping her, but really, I was putting off seeing Mum.

Mum needed lots of room in the car, as her leg is in plaster and she has crutches to lean on. As they pulled into the street, they could see the banner, clearly declaring to the world, in rainbow colours,

WE LOVE YOU MUM!

When the car stopped, people poured out of the house to greet her. I hung back. Dad helped her to her feet and supported her as she tried to walk. She looked up at the banner, and all around at the crowd of smiling faces.

'Thank you, everyone. This is so amazing. That banner, it's beautiful. What a lovely surprise, thank you.' She hugged Nat. Then she saw me. She put her arms out to me. After a momentary hesitation, I moved forward and let her hug me.

Nat was so excited. 'Eve helped us make the banner. In fact, the whole thing was her idea.'

'Not really. The girls did most of it,' Eve said, blushing.

'It's wonderful.' Mum smiled, turning back to Eve. 'Thank you.'

'Come on, let's go inside and eat loads of food and dance!' announced Eve. 'Ah, or maybe just eat,' she said, looking at Mum on crutches.

The food was great. There was loads of it. Everyone was making yummy noises over Eve's cakes. Most people were mingling and chatting and fussing over Mum. Not many were dancing, I have to say, just Nat and her friends. Even they were mainly giggling and falling on the floor. Dad was chatting to Mum. They were sitting on the sofa, watching Nat's antics and laughing as they talked. They looked like old friends. I couldn't figure them out.

Eve caught me watching them. She put her arm round my shoulder. 'Time to make up with your Mum yet?'

I nodded. Despite what she'd done, she's still my Mum and I love her. I walked across to her and Dad. She looked up and smiled, then I just gave her a great big hug.

'Thank you,' she whispered.

Eve was back in the kitchen, talking to lots of different people, and making sure everyone was okay for drinks. The whole day was weird. Zoe was talking to her about the wedding and the letter and all the stuff I didn't want her to bring up right now.

I backed off, but Zoe saw me and followed. 'She's pretty cool you know.'

'What makes you say that?' I said, thinking of all the horrible things Zoe had spouted about Evil Eve over the past few weeks.

'Well, after what your Mum did. I know she had her reasons, and I don't blame her. But, Eve's been so great about it.' Then with a twinkle in her crazy eyes, she said, 'In fact, you could say she's been a WICKED stepmother!'

I gave her the look, then, at the same time, we both cackled...

MWAH-HAH-HAH-HAAAH!

Another letter from Lou

Hi again,

Some of you might be going through a tough time with your family, at the moment, or maybe you know someone who is. It was tough for me, but it was good to have people to talk to about it. And my sense of humour kept me going too.

If you want to talk to other people who might understand how you're feeling, there are organisations you can contact. One of these is Childline.

www.childline.org.uk - Telephone 0800 1111

Remember to stay safe online!
I hope this helps.

Love,

Lou

About Karen ...

Karen lives near York with her husband and two children. One of her favourite things to do as a child, was to draw lots of stick families and make up stories about them. It's a good job she is a writer now, not an illustrator!

When Karen was a teacher, part of her job was helping children to be able to express their feelings and emotions in a positive way. This inspired her to write a book to prompt conversations about difficult circumstances young people might find themselves in.

Karen loves to hear from readers and always replies to emails. Please contact her via our website.

Other books from GoApe Junior and Teenage Fiction:

Knights of the Wobbly Table
Fairy Rescuers
Return to Elysia
Breaking Silence

Other publications from Monkey Island:

Angel Small
Angel Small Follows the Star
Angel Small The Musical

About Gill ...

Gill has illustrated and designed many children's books, and is delighted to have teamed up with Karen to bring a whole new perspective to her portfolio.

Gill was brought up in rural Lancashire and spent most of her childhood drawing and exploring the hills and streams in wellies. To this day she maintains an interest in all things wiggly. Her most beloved places are hilly and woody, so living in the Yorkshire Dales is most enjoyable, especially with her husband and two children.

Together Gill and Karen
have created Monkey Island Publishing
to bring you stories in word, pictures and song.
For more information, go to:

www.monkeyislandpublishing.com